THE
RAGGED
VERTICAL

THE
RAGGED
VERTICAL

HARRY E. NORTHUP

3-11-96
JONATHAN,
    YOU ARE A BRILLIANT
AMERICAN DIRECTOR +
I AM HONORED TO HAVE
WORKED WITH YOU. THANKS
FOR YOUR FINANCIAL HELP
ON THIS BOOK. BEST TO
JOANNE.
        love,
        Harry

cahuenga
PRESS

ACKNOWLEDGMENTS & PERMISSIONS

Acknowledgments: Some of these poems have appeared in *L.A. Weekly; Pearl; Hollywood Magazine; ONTHEBUS; Barney;"Poetry Loves Poetry": An Anthology of Los Angeles Poets; Grand Passion: The Poets of Los Angeles and Beyond; Bachy; Zephyr; Angry Candy; Contrast;* and on the poetry CD and cassette recordings, "Personal Crime" and "Homes" (both released by New Alliance Records).

The author is indebted to the following for permission to reprint copyrighted work: Edward Dorn; Robert Creeley; Gary Snyder; Donald Allen, executor for Lew Welch; Robert Duncan:*The Opening of the Field.* Copyright © 1960 by Robert Duncan. Reprinted by permission of New Directions Publishing Corp.; Ebbe Borregaard; Denise Levertov: *Collected Earlier Poems* 1940-1960. Copyright © 1959 by Denise Levertov. Reprinted by permission of New Directions Publishing Corp.; Philip Lamantia; Allen Ginsberg; Jack Spicer: *The Collected Books of Jack Spicer*, published by Black Sparrow Press; Ray Bremser; Frank O'Hara, permission of Grove Press; Jack Kerouac, permission of Grove Press; Peter Orlovsky; Barbara Guest; Philip Walen; Stuart Z. Perkoff, permission by Gerald T. Perkoff, M.D.

ISBN 0-9649240-0-5

Front cover photo: Don Lewis
Typesetting: Greg Boyd
This book was printed at McNaughton & Gunn, Inc., Saline, MI.

Cahuenga Press is owned, financed and operated by its poet-members James Cushing, Phoebe MacAdams, Harry E. Northup, Holly Prado Northup, Cecilia Woloch. Our common goal is to create fine books of poetry by poets whose work we admire and respect; to make poetry actual in the world in ways which honor both individual creative freedom and cooperative support.

Cahuenga Press
1256 N. Mariposa Ave.
Los Angeles, CA 90029

For Holly Prado Northup & Dylan Northup

CONTENTS

HUMILITIES
2-1-89 to 6-20-90

the ragged vertical
12-5-90 to 12-27-91

265 — EXT. PLAZA HOTEL — NIGHT

7-22-75
to
9-26-75

& there is child support & film, yes, a brief
scene at the st. regis, where marty lives—
the bellmore cafeteria (in three years there
won't be a fleet cab on the street)

                                        st. mark's
cinema, two scorsese films

                7   22   1975

prometheus you are worthy stone you desire
fame cadillacs horns suns wine & benign& elegant
ladies

prometheus you are more handsome on cocaine

                7   27   1975

she thinks you are crazy because you sit by the
window
a window that has an excellent view of a blue sky
4 car stalls a roof & telephone lines
where i have never seen bluejays
where sometimes a ball bounces
because you write poems calling her aphrodite
& yourself eros &

what about the hostage compassion
is

8   6   1975

its your physical movement that must be seen
entering & to come back the thought forward
45th, or was it 44th, & 10th, the st. regis
20th & 6th avenue, the firing range downstairs
light rain, smoke out of the subways, a honk,
a yellow cab running a red light
you are safe when you are led by a master.
after all, movies are fame, no film is trans-
parent. film is harvey keitel & bette midler
discussing fanny brice & billy rose.
accentuate the syncopate.
"film is visual," said martin scorsese.

9 killings in one 24 hour period.
one lover was shot through a peep hole.
& 2 were suicide related, then they follow
you & track you: the pain the hand holds.
& primary colors, each scene a different choice
to wear, its all a magic act, who can remember.
allow the schizophrenia for the 10 minutes before
after all, film is a director's medium, he hired
you & he trusts you, he wants you to step out,
don't let them peg you, never repeat yourself.
i never once heard a raised voice.
the problem is money when you have a deadline.
& the week before ruffian died, & the week after

billy jean king won, & i wore a ruffian button
i wore it to exploit his desire to win, he won.
a romantic purist. who? scorsese.

8   9   1975

names my poems are full of names
last night i called laguna information
& got diane wakoski's phone number
i felt like making love to her early poems

8   19   1975

i went over to eldons house to get a j he was
showering doesnt that chick sheila have a great
body shes beautiful shes sexy shes open
but then we started talking about time
breathless starts at 8 30 shall we go early
enough to sing about jesus or time to eat mexican
food
she has been asking for grey matter again & again
mickey mouse at least 4 times & to me though
where do you go after a man can make you laugh &
cry

14

who are the trailblazers in new york all wait
underground otherwise you will fall
he wanted to fuck her & she digs me he wants to
ask her to go see breathless tonight maybe we will
stay for week-end the last chick was in my house
when i came home
my face is all cut its the darkness under your eyes
there are mountains & the lines are drawn
theres no way to lose weight like cocaine
what about the chick shes working i have to get a
duplicate of a sink & mirror my fantasy
sleeps after & then the security of the framed
reality its just that the films of the fifties
streetcar was an influence their sense of reality
was this the way it was that phony an extreme
apartment near cooper sq lets steal even if we
have to steal

8   19   1975

bill my life has to be changed radically i
want to thank you for deciding to publish the
cock of jesus & eros ash together
lee said it was genius

however for the second & last time i have to
say again i have decided not to publish the
cock of jesus it is my best work contained

emotionally i cannot accept its consequences

i have no purpose
i do have a choice
a direction if i can ever accept thought
these poems are dreams in the evernothing of
dreams he imitates me my son when he sleeps
he dreams naked the nights along the ocean
that man is passive that man sits in his room

totally & irreducible apolitical & existentially
memory & saint paul is the mind of the university
woman is the spirit behind the city

8   19   1975

promethean desire to be loaded constantly
sure zeus was beat
fire will you support my cock while i fuck
astro-turf
grey-matter
desire to be vicarious itself
let's settle the grey-matter
has there been a cinematic flash since the new wave
the french have no heroes
an artificial tree so lifelike it's unreal
the difference between life & reality
                exploit the illuminati—
benign diamond
desire opens a gate & walks up a path around until
astonishing steps downward
looking for the two houses seen from the top

let's steal even if we have to steal—
words honor
do you know much about proust?
no, only the rumors

brandos making up for lost time, there was a time
when existentialism said dont give a shit &
those whose argument was the reaching out remains
genet? genet would kiss my ass before i would
kiss his, & then the 60s believed it, 10 years
went by, all of a sudden we must give a shit, or
else well get snuffed so he began to give a shit
not me, i happen to like all of brandos films,
like kazan, did you like the arrangement? i did
while she played a guitar on an island, another
girl had an affair, like sometimes someone hands
me a book & it influences me, there are no great
20c film critics, they can only deal with what
went on in front of the camera, where is the cor-
relation to the whole star
she looked so inviting, standing naked in front
of me, i love to iron, i love to cook, i have 2
children, didnt you love, when do you learn the
affair, the movie affair, it takes 2, when you
enter a room with a whore you dont fuck her &
she doesnt fuck you, most underground film happen
s behind the camera

8   25   1975

17

yes man shot u; rowing, spend, more, with, &
sight in him, he must, you, cannot, the, now
when, lost white, his distance, they, chief,
power base, half, civil, gone past, buried
free, when enter, d end &, take down the i,
thought, i am my own, image, truth be, bet.
light, past, the. future, did you get the
necessity times, release. the violence had
to come out. when you hit, she stood inviti
ng. an argue, america, an eagle, when, we,
know across listen only lit, a slight, i
have to remain, was the horse, won. a male
or a female, the light, 1 won, 1 dead, a
romantic, burst, purist 10, & lost & dead,
by desire 2 won, & buried, they went, 1 min-
ute a moment ago, we wondered why, i waited.
all the women along, & lived with bass, ,
long vowel, they forget to compare the re-
visionists must it always plus memory, when
violent fucking, wonderful

8   25   1975

barbara miller called me on my 35th birthday
250 a day, a fork lift operator, 1 day,
bogart slept here, with de niro & mike nichols
barbara, i just finished taxi driver with
scorsese & de niro in new york, a featured role
its a scene with de niro, a confrontation,
no, i need the bread, fine, 250 a day is all

we can pay, sound stage 14, warner brothers,
12 30 to see nichols.
my birthday, i gave rita the 70 dollars child
support, stopped in westwood to walk around
& see a movie.
ran into 2 cab drivers at lums, reynolds went
back with his wife, he lives below rush in
the projects, hes having a party thursday night
went & saw coonskin, wonderful & flawed,
hes the only one since disney, but bambi is a
great film, bought pears & a wineglass, & white
grape juice, woke & washed my hair & shaved.
i ran into de niro at the break for lunch
hey bobbie, hi harry, i enjoyed working with
you in new york, bobbie. me, too. what are
you here for? they called me last night, some-
thing about a fork lift operator, a scene with
you. oh yeah, where he asks for directions.
maybe, i should see the a d.
this is harry northup.
well, they dont need you but i will tell him
you are a friend of de niros.
sorry, harry
see you.

9   3   1975

the end. its bed, unmade, gods, even electri-
city, she cannot keep the books. i mean,
when i work, my sex drive goes down. the click
came before you heard, are you going to make it

parody, 1 laugh, a black button. i suspect
novelists whose books are always made into movies.
you are ambitious, how fast the songs
came, he mentioned jung & flying saucers.
your car must be moved in the morning, alarm.
the end of printing, the end of personal faith.
its personal beyond. in the frame of. a hair,
it cannot be stopped by a door, why are you
parking in my parking spot, why does he leave
because he heard you talking & comparing
an old iranian myth about walls dimension.
anything people please, except, murder.
how can you stop yourself from the pain
stopped him in the 5th. a boxer carried my
suitcase to the greyhouund bus. after your
mothers death, you never go back, am i respon-
sible for the pain my wife bears when she hates
to work as a secretary, when my child has diffi
-culty speaking long sentences, i hate long sen
-tences, i love peaches, she saw the childrens
faces turn from white to black, she called a
cab from the asylum, no one home, i collected
from her twice, once as a deposit before leav-
ing the airport, no one home at 4 am, in azusa
i saw a car on the curb, put her 3 bags in &
said get in, & lock the door

9   7   1975

sheila

we had a wonderful weekend coked out
swimming smoking listening to joan baez sing
love songs to bobbie dylan
when sheila met a mystic the mystic said
i will kiss you as soon as i go around the wall
i did not know there was a wall said sheila
it has moved me twice in two years & both the
chicks were crazy one said as we were fucking
please do not let the other men fuck me
i am very vulnerable
                                i am coming over do you
want me to ring before i come
should i give you a buzz before i come
one said you shot me in the heart with your
castle

9   8   1975

where is his belt? his shoes were on backwards,
should i kiss you good-bye? no, that will come
later, a wheel rolling toward the wooden gate
i will watch him tuesday, after lunch, till thurs
day evening. you have to get his glasses friday.
i have a dentist apt at 4 45, after work.
then, too. choo choo great funny face, he loves
his skateboard, movies, red wagon, match box
cars, popcorn & coke, & lucy, flintstones, dennis
the menace; he hates football, loves surfing,
then, teaching is the attempt to lie, i bought

21

the belt, she had a backwards day, the moment i
heard a motorcycle i shut the window, it is pain
to know that he has no consciousness to
know what it is, to be unable to speak,
at his will, the will releases its need, i need
your body & my mind to release, how can you
teach anything but withdrawal, the need marshals
my father was a man who read pocketbooks &
drank beer, went for the morning paper daily at
7 15, up for 2 hours, a glass of beer at boyd's
cigar store, i fell drunk on our living room
floor, 17, the truth the whole cunt, nothing
but the cock, & marriage abstracts pain.
there is a severed head in the hatbox, if you
say there is a severed head in the hatbox, you
believe, a 4 story, deep lawns, a lake, with
white chairs, the chairs lounge like hoodlums,
i love to take my time when i shave.

9   8   1975

killkiss poetsdoor ran
stairs, heard she called, he walked over, she sat
on a bench along the path to the zoo on a sunday.
it has to be a dream, you read the words, a man &
a woman, a child, an attempt to be a leader, by
buying time where all the energy is, its film, sad.
other girl do you want to get it on with her.
dollar bills in the homegrown on the paino, hat &
cane, left it is she who offers i should have

sheets, shutters, white phone, white rug,

piano, satin sheets, waiting for day winds, my god
stealing cars, destroying rural school houses, sy-
phoning gas at midnight from farmers near the lin-
coln highway, picking potatoes, moving every year,
the good thing about you as a poet is that you are
not afraid to lie, one brother out of three, one
sister, you need it for your work, what is its pur-
pose. to witness. its wetness. its clothing.
my friend lied, they made the father stand up to
apologize. for the son. we must dedicate pleasure
to the moment we are at each other's feet about
to enter each other with our tongue.

                    9   13   1975

there is no other time than now & now is
the time of the romantic purist, the romantic
purist has the anonymity of de niro, the
darkest grain romanus, he was hired because of
the way he picked up his cigarette lighter:
sleek, the angle between the unloading the
lenses, the conflict to be bought, when he arr
ived at the train station jaglom dressed him
in a porter's outfit, a host, one girl said
she could not believe him as a porter, he was
too handsome, no one is as handsome as aprea,
scorsese, cooper, jack kerouac, de niro is the
best actor, he believes he can be anybody.
handsome as the beat poets.
handsome as henry miller & anais nin.

handsome as frank corsaro's acting class.
handsome as ann stanford's pure poetry.
handsome as complete & harmony.
handsome as robert rossen directing lilith.
handsome as every howard hawks film has a girl
singing next to a piano.
handsome as warren oates in a white suit.
handsome as mean streets.
handsome as breathless.
handsome as taxi driver.

9   13   1975

when you kill someone with a knife

its work
its like fucking someone.

9   22   1975

she never wears panties when she wears a dress
heat night void sandals.

9   26   1975

24

1980

spring

clear raw wind
far clean
interrupt blood
fertile awaken-
ing
father grand
on wall
above blackboard
kindergarten
memory
like a signature
on a check
ready captive
white borders
what is story?
finding order
friends cause
the discussion
led talks
good that might
thrill completely
star of beginning
own blessing
emotion fire
rain warmth
perpetual fertility
woman wearing
sky protect
where wind follows
raging violet
kiss a bleeding
window amnesty
how deep is revenge
the whole heaven
is so full of water

3   28   1980

boy with three surfboards

red biboveralls & yellow red hair
woman with tan sitting behind the boy

poet teacher gray black hair
tree & mountain behind her in the frame
cuts off her shoulders

man with short haircut
white shirt too big
woman with permanent

three strawberries
horse kicking above the ocean that begins
green star
naked woman with one red leg one black leg

blonde young girl with blond
young boy
in field of tall grasses

boy in blue biboveralls & wearing sandals
standing in an art gallery in venice
woman nude
below her breasts to above her knees

four actors playing new york cabbies
sitting at two tables in a west side cafe
rainy lights

photograph of a man with free press & 25¢
covering the left side of his upper head
review of a book of poetry cutting off
his right eye & the rest of his face

woman with black hair
green neck & blood red left shoulder
green & red cover the hieroglyphs
instead of using the alphabet
it simply frames a figure with red
under a right eye without color

two simply white figures
a woman with flesh colored circles
lines indented & lines extended up
word connected with gray & blue
no line between the whiteness

4   14   1980

poem to women

there is no greater energy than writing poem
there is no greater energy than making love
than fucking than waking than holding than releasing
there is no greater thing than woman
there is no nor no nothing no anything as great as anything
nothing is greater than man
than woman with man than man with child than woman who
gives affection to woman
there is no greater earth
there is no greater love poem to islam
than this love for women for boys for ocean for sky for nothing
ever has anything less than giving away nothing less than love
for woman

4 19 1980

a tremendous depression i heard

today is a fair at john muir
gray for the past two days
it went away like clouds & rain
the fucking was hot as fire
prometheus & bride making light
hawaiian shirt & altered wranglers
the boy read strong & clear
strong as a noun a place to where
he had come with exercise & routine
study
baskets of wealth passed to spending
for hiding & receiving at the appropriate
time with no wanting more
the fastness of fire breaking
a past so fragile we change our minds
from goodness to darkness
over the thought of another giving
to another
& the many minds
tonight i would like to see
a senseless movie
fair & food & entertainment
the in's & out's an entry
disloyal & disgraces
being part of something
in this case working in one's field
the three days a cause for secureness
a slowness beyond real time
listening & hearing finally
waves two & three times hitting the shore
in between sentences
sometimes in between words
looking the other actor

right in the eye
taking time to come out of the darkness
where no one can see anything
so speed is certainly nonessential
"you make me feel like a swan"
burning up & then sleep
friday morning in hollywood
i read a trade paper & a newspaper
the external world had no effect
on me i was too busy including the fire
from last night the fire light
a good night's sleep
& a good light's love is holy answer
clouds & rain & gets warmer blue

4   29   1980

it was a time that came upon

wealth & all his friends.
in a doom , it did not last long.
for all to see .a beginning.
authentic
hate broke down & cried
snapped a photograph at its object
denying
courage, stood squarely
looked another straight in the face.
james cagney said
"hit your marks
& look the other actor straight
in the eyes."
what did, was, an another who gave
regeneration.
thought one was lost to a moral code
like conrad
or the bible
a code of ethics is simply
belonging to field & loneliness
what is not what should be or ought.
like a nuclear scientist
like a field biologist
like a poet.
into a deep plumage of language
to carry the river through.
through names, incidents sexual appetite.
with all its doom with names of others
seeing only with words
in the fields of carrying
carrying past deeds into the present
steps toward meaning are discarded by religious
seeing them unnecessary in the face of reaching
goodness

meaning exactly as one says
trying to catch up what is past
in any contradiction.
a right exists, not in a battle of opposites.
nor in logic, nor in loneliness, nor outside
human language.
arguments over content & form.
as if one could exist in a land of argument.
any school child knows
"poetry comes from the heart."

5   12   1980

messenger killing

heroin is the daddy
heroin is the boss
no matter how much money you got
or how high your position
you start heroin
& heroin is all you think about
two things with heroin
1   the shooting
2   the drug
seeing the blood come into the syringe
knowing you hit a vein
shoot in & count
one to ten & if you hit ten you know
that you are alive
if you hit four & thats all
you re dead
but you dont think about death
heroin getting more of it
everything is directed toward heroin
thats all you think about is heroin

lenny bruce s end came when he got
started up with the catholic church
the head dude in each city s catholic church
cracked down on the police force
all lenny asked for was
for a definition of what obscenity was
his last rap was about jesus & moses
what if they came to earth today

what is meaning
thats what a junkie asks himself over & over
take all your worries & magnify them thousands of times

heroin takes you straight to oblivion
no more worries
oblivion

have they taken your freedom away from them
heroin
shooting & watching the blood
come into the syringe
talking about madness
that never comes back
holes where they put the drugs

5   12   1980

to understand modern poetry

to understand modern poetry
you have to understand that ginsberg goes back through blake
through shakespeare to the prophets of the old testament
isiah jeremiah micah, add an a for faith in the middle of the
first name
that the waste land of eliot is simply a collage of western
literature cut up & put together
he studied sanskrit but not too far or too deep so that he
could remain in the frame work of western civilization
someone asked gandhi what he thought of western civilization
& gandhi said "what civilization?"
randall jarrell's war poems are strongly authentic
to understand modern poetry
you have to realize that e e cummings was our middle class poet
singing songs of middle small towns throughout america
blake's jerusalem is a sensuous body of language
if i were a critic i would write an essay on ann stanford's
the weathercock holly prado's feasts & wanda coleman's mad dog
black lady & creeley for love
crane's the bridge & hd with a space & two periods has exquisite
control
the music of g. stein & how hemingway & her affected each other
the long poems of pound & zukofsky & wcwilliams & eliot's four
quartets a shaft of light turning perimeters around a blooming
quiet still time
could someone remain a poet without mentioning the paris review
the black mountain poets a birth of many women writers an unusual
amount of drugs used in the psychology of craft never before
the same in acting along with stanislavski & strasberg an unusual
amount of talking & discussing the aesthetics of what it takes
to balance a structure & the entrance of the orient through trans-
lations & gary snyder & phil whalen & how much hart crane
                                        rebelled

against the waste land
to understand modern poetry
one must understand waste & fission & fusion & neutron
& einstein
marx freud jung the quantum theory & we live in a very gnostic
time so one must understand pluralities & rothenberg's "multi-
tribal" world
non-objective painting the surrender to a subjective joy a bewild-
ering & delicious unity that prescribes shadows to selves rejoices
many women many children many workers many men many
useful hands
the marxist theory has brought the printing press into the hands
or surrender a comprehensiveness

5   19   1980

language

language west
open love
bewilder please
depend upon
many with flowers

hungry flaws
waves &waves
flinched when
he began preaching
four white people
in a black church
dancing blood
singing loud &
lively the way
the young should

it took a long while
to sit still
after looking upward
hope was spoken about
spirit also
we sheltered each
memory providing
sanctuary from
flesh worries

language turned
to its neighbor
shook hands
each said to each
i love you

the first time
i said i love you
to a man
at the same time
a man said i love you
to me waking away
a cold deliberate
religious heart
quietly we spoke

never before a church
like that
prayers full of singing
an inner reaching up
to receive a lighter
spirit than exists
in ration
neighbor near &within
quiet speaking love

6   3   1980

sports

ted williams was my boyhood idol
i read *sport* magazine & *ring*
baseball every summer morning at ten
with other boys from the depot
little league, midgets, pony league,
jr league, semi-pro
& i never played in any form of a league again

basketball in the snow
played with gloves on
we lived twelve miles from town
on an army depot
the high school was in town
& i played jr high basketball, freshman, &
high school
as a junior, i was 6th, 7th, or 8th man
five starters or four starters & a sub got kicked off
for breaking training rules & i became a starter
when i was a senior i got kicked off for drinking
puking at the senior cotillion
drunk while with the french exhange student
genevieve abougie
i took her to the winter dance & fell drunk on the high
school lawn & puked in the auditorium
went home in the early morning & smashed the glass
in the upper door & reached through & opened the door
from the inside i had lost my key & fell down on the
living room floor
that was when i decided to join the navy at a ripe old
age of 17, when i might add, i got kicked out of being
lt. gov., of being sports editor of the h.s. paper, out
of honor society, out of being pres. of the drama club,
& i had to apologize to the entire senior class

in less than a month i will be 40
these days when i get a part in a movie i go play
basketball in a nearby park
i must have a purpose

photographs of whiteness
that was then & this is now
the first part of the paper i read
in the morning is the sports section
playing basketball with gloves on
baseball every morning in the summer
a group of boys ready to play

august 6, 1980

be a real daylight

dont come to my door
with your i dont remember
memory was never so real
you never saw anything so
damned open

8 6 80

theory

i had this theory rather inner need about loss
evidently it had been language syllables
indo european through mouths of stones across
northern everlasting to bridge water & race
carrying being carried the sound of spanish
horses

into my childhood of baseball community theatre
basketball holding hands with a girl in a movie
theatre
clock to the side of the screen
evidently it all had a message
waiting for the right time when i would reach out
hold her hand the time when i had enough nerve

it was to say that drive ins swimming pools beaches
lawns walks houses cars hold man & woman in love
holds woman & woman in love holds man & man in love
& the atomic bombs go off in my mind & the middle
eastern wars go off in my mind &
still i read by natural light that is what i enjoy
doing most in the morning sitting by a window
evidently there is structuring & most likely
woman first by woman & man he by first
we came out of woman just like we came out of indo
european & we came out of woman just like a tree
rises from the earth from the earth a seed & it
takes time to rise from a womb & never want to go back
regression say the great blue cloud who place no ration
in thought understanding an unconscious desire to love
it was a love of language that brought me to woman
man & woman had been nomads
into the center of the plains in the heart from the
northern part of the largest

our ignorance is such we still do not know what the financiers
are doing with our money
womans intuition said to man
kill those people & lets move on
& man did the killing because he
had always been the one who went out to bring in
there is too much for the computer to hold
i sit by the window & wonder whether it matters who desires
killing first
whether i blame you for the wars as if your ability to civilize
has often come at a time when the horses have defined movement
from earth like a seed to bend forward with woman
who works her field not like a man but woman like
like a seed defining earth a language returning

brother

he calls me brother
& i do deeds for him
simply because
he asked me

as he gets out
of my car he turns
"i buy you with dope"
"i love myself more
than i love you"
he lets me watch
channel z
at his house
when he is gone

he gives me direction
helps me with affection
gives me ideas
overflows from himself

he wants to weigh
what he got for me
open it first display it
friend with physical
helpfulness

he says women dont want
men as friends
tells me about incest
brother says he felt
her desire for him
in a room with her once
old hotel castle beach

brother looks past
what stands in front
why did i come to the beach
if he isnt here
& when he gets out he doesnt
call to let me know hes out
i run into him & we each eat
a hamburger with coffee
two bucks each with tip

he calls me brother
i do deeds for him
& hope i dont get caught

8   6   80

my brother came to town

my brother came to town
i picked him up at the los angeles airport
drive him east on century to normandie
to 3500 s normandie to a church
where he stayed from tuesday afternoon
till thursday at one
thursday at one i picked him up at the church
drove to long beach where he bought flowers
on to bertha gertison's apartment
in long beach
talked with her for several hours
talk about the dust bowl
our family lived in colorado then
the dust thick & a hundred feet up it rises
a big rectangle rocks spinning out hitting
her arms the dust so thick prarie dogs digging
trying to dig themselves out a hundred feet
in the air
she knew me when i was just born
bertha was an occupational therapist
at the northwest hospital in amarillo
where my dad worked where i was born
she was dying of cancer
in her eighties she said one of these days i'll
just fade away
then we drove down the coast to visit a high school
classmate of my brother
we stopped at "the glider" a seafood restaurant
on coast highway in seal beach that has airplanes
hanging from its ceiling an inexpensive good sea-
food restaurant
it has been there for fifty years & in the early
years of its existence there was a glider factory

across from it
he paid for dinner
then we drove to huntington beach where jim bolita
& his wife "billie" live
jim & my brother graduated from high school in 1942
i got dizzy from all the names thrown around & all
the old photos & talk of class mates identifying
them by how much hair they have in recent photos
& distant meetings
polaroid photos were taken
two of my brother & me
one for each
i drove him to the traveler's lodge by the airport
walked him to the elevator & said "i love you, bobbie"

8   7   80

dear martha

dear martha
the cool mornings are best these hot days but the last
three days have been uncomplaining about weather matters
what matters is i have been reading writing sleeping
during the strike eating conversing also feeling very
disconnected from something i had worked for & on in
preparing the time a month & more
books i have been reading are notes from underground &
rilke& norton anthology of modern poetry & one with
painters & poets many new york ones
& to my right are many paintings the one in front a beau-
tiful bursting yellow & orange with red under & blues
greens light pushed out from a white tennis shoe without
laces delapidated in its flatness the flatness of emotion
with a round red ball on its inner ankle side blue shoe-
string holes & a red above a blue stripe around the edge
of the bottom top part of the inch around to go up
& once i thought it was just sleeping & worrying &
waiting then a green little rocking chair with a red cap
a blue & white cap a gray sport cap from detroit hanging
a picture of my mother & father gray near death his white
shirt too big around his neck a new haircut for him a
permanent for her hair
my brother said when they got old they both had sugar di-
abetes i knew my father did & he said one of the medicines
being injected was later found to be no good & was one of
the causes of each of their deaths
& then a book of photographs from 20s & 30s one a woman
on horseback bareback with wheat fields in the background
my aunt on horseback in kansas
memory is youthful my mother was gray when i was in high

school & in these pictures she is as beautiful as a dark
smile holding a woman with black short hair a curl at her
forehead holding her first born
i was the fifth three boys & a girl all older
basketball red wagon blue desk brown notebook script call
sheet union strike letter a book on zen
i hear the gardener outside & i turn to the window with
its white roads & red stars green leaves downward from
a womans body
he is gone for a minute & then he is back & i turn to the
red wagon in the corner blocking the door
its handle close to a dictionary
& may you have sunshine & may you have many breezes
                                                          from
the lady whose ravens gather again & again we follow the
loneliness from nothing but a far away woman working
a letter not to sum up or reach for or hold but this waiting
a month into summer while occupied by a strike
dear martha from harry in west hollywood love

                              8   7   80

ordinary language & praise

praise rivers with bridges
with bridges overflowing
going through a river city
on a greyhound
seeing them prepare for a
rising
kissing a young runaway girl
in the back seat of the bus
praise flowers that open sooner
than thought would
have to be depended upon
praise them quick to insult
& quick to be paranoid
praise magazines with heroes
praise strike that threw me
out of work
praise the whole & the whole
that does not look out for the
one who struck for the whole
praise stinginess cowardice
praise every once in a while
a student has an inspiring
teacher
praise woman who loves works shares
cooks cleans shelters opens
praise closes
praise eternity great plains sage-
teeth claws mind eyebrow cheekbone
praise young man an affirmation of
hope a new bone never found old
praise toughness & overcoat worn
in eastern northern cold city
praise the broken & the healing

in a strike that i did not vote for
i hurt from
the loss of income of unemployment
praise walked off the job voluntarily
praise pleases aloneness
praise work and praise it hard
praise worm & praise corn cow & hoe
praise money from home when young
praise feeding ones own
praise grief for a loss of love
praise time there is time to carry one
through
praise those who carry stone to block
praise like a river out of control
filled with what envy prays for

8   18   80

what am i supposed to do then

thee a one thought in each rising sickness sorrow
this external pain causes
                              returning to you to speak sorrow
an existential learning devotion to constantly examining
daylight drugs
that one & request descriptions what make of car
two men killed four persons in west los angeles
i get to be the cat & then a rat
                              denying the fact that i
arrest the words some god damn mysterious spirit
escapes into the dread of seeing a guard
what am i supposed to be then
a fucking servant
                      i speak sorrow to examine sorrow
& then you return upon me & i dont get time to spend with
the ocean & walk upon a pier to get out & go upon
is it from not eating
another calls & says not enough vitamins in his body
& i think to help i understand to try to help another
begin again & i fail
                          & then i am not with myself trying
to understand & help another & each of us demands much
what am i supposed to then
i go with you to escape myself dream anothers dream get lost
get lost in another losing oneself in drugs movies acting
writing loving peaceful ocean a ravaged lonely time when i
am by myself i will do anything to lose myself
& then when i'm like a cat i go into the back bedroom
having only the bedroom light on & enjoying being by myself
if anyone knocks i wont answer
then later comparing myself to those who inherit great society
their gracious attractiveness an intellect among animal beauty
but then you ask me & i go i too get tired alone from aloneness
we need sharing as our friendship

begin to fall i again fall into sleep & sit by the window
reading when i first wake
what am i supposed to be then
be alone when writing before writing to have time to suffer
this sickening aloneness & this sickening need to have time
alone to have quietness because society is too big & loud
at times for me & time helps rebuild regather winds within the
heart in which at all times man has found solace
from the outer taking away

8   26   1980

the sickness got past

even love has doubts
in the middle walking
sureness decides whom
shall pass closest
without touching

shall be formed
resolutely & with honor
it is enough to reach
out, with kindness
she denies

sickness has money
not the same way again
talk about an inner life
refines pragmatism
we are born by

gentle with greenery
certain side of the family
every love has wisdom
blindness born to lose
heading north in rain

shall we lose our thoughts
in love a night alone
cleanliness to come
sickness & crying
born through born through

in a sickness crying
love shall be born
whereby we lose ourselves

keeping recording
for our own sanity

shall we lose our nights
in love
i am born to waking
early mornings in summer
resolutely & in like manner

above a union relies
shelter heart an upcoming
hotness blueness a closing
for losing all love
this union reborn love

8   28   1980

past perfect

i walk past him in the end
into a coolness
i walk past her in the end
past her into coolness
an affording sadness
comes a time when i say
take your car take your stories
leave me alone
all your efforts at equal specifics
an equality of conditions
where we talk about favorite colors
it beats me to death
god was an invention of the poor
sure god was beat
but why d they have to advertise it so
going around the corner to death
how much can you carry in your pocket
hold in your hand
into what for how much
i walk past you & leave you reading
for entering & never speaking
giving only material things
well if we are going to talk about values
we might as well talk about things
i walk past sickness i walk past sorrow
i walk with love past love
aggressive as well as quiet a sensibility
without names
fighters defenders honor will come out
when needed
in the connections are there unity
with barely enough money for food
money for two months rent
i walk & i have walked i have had to walk

with nothing for nothing with anything &
it got to be strength to go on with nothing
nothing that wasnt prepared among the many
surprises

8   28   1980

its getting crazy

its getting crazy
the birthday party was fine
i am the angel of fun
we listened to jazz
& i drove to your home twice
leaving you finally at a cafe
in the valley
& then i shut my door
to stop the music from above
waking feeling stuffy
& then it sickens me
the darkness
that i fled
with poverty
1)   a man praised me
2)   a man bought for me
3)   a man criticized me
4)   a man rode with me
5)   a man painted
when i go to the museum
i like to meditate
the girl sitting behind us
she was nice
the tickets were green
& the others had orange tickets
the guard let us in
color he kept saying was what
painting was all about
not the story
that i kept talking about
trying to figure out
which figure in the painting
was jesus & what about
the snakes in the upper right corner

he said look at the brown background
how it moves in on the body
of the naked woman
japanese prints true respect
he got me into the museum free
& he bought me custard & coffee
two of his new paintings
have flowers growing out of the wall
hot plate instant coffee
a stem without grapes
the grapes eaten the stem left

9   3   80

america

so put me on hold baby
you are greater than i thought you were
you were capable of
a sunburst
a minorah
a candle burning
you are the crown of the statue
of liberty
spirals & jackson pollock striding across western
europe
a boy from an immediate love
the statue of liberty wears a skirt of freeways

& then we fight & then we point hold
then we fuck then we kiss every night before saying
i love you
& then i am so tired i can hardly bear to continue holding
all that you have given me
thinking of ed dorn & paul blackburn & leland hickman &
yourself a great beauty
the blonde north listen a freedom of speech
you never exclude me & you include all wars
pluralities skidding across freeway lanes
crashing into the center
from whence we came we came out of the water
the women loving women say we came from women
from mother fuck father
kill the mother fuck the father

looks like you were right
you came along just at the right time to pull me out of
isolation in the big city on the pacific coast
i come to you for comfort
something that we can both share

u.s. detail
a polite society
remembers us all & has patience to refuse begin again exclusion
& i sleep in your bosom & watch the fast jets
you are jet ace number one

                                        10   6   80

solitude

what willful-
act precedes
happiness in
finding new
beauty
with our legs,
our thighs, our
bodies pulling
towards each
other with another
who loves you
as much &more
she having a more
intimate longevity
i do not want to
interrupt, i
half listen, half
watch &listen to
men & women stand-
ing near
getting to know you
more, we dress for
each other
looking forward
to meeting, still
a little bit shy
some are meant
to be near
how much i wanted
to say i like the fur
around the upper half
of your body
how much i wanted

to say
you are beautiful to-
night
how you said something
about how it is no good
to hate the opposite
when many were discussing
darkness
we got closer tonight.

12   15   80

LOSS
3-17-85
to
8-18-85

loss

i painted over the gangs' names
& the bad names the rival gangs
called each other
in this area because each live
on this street, one at each end
& there is a girl in the middle
patch work

my son has been gone for six days
& the coldness stumbles into eternity
love & dismay, sadness
blame, happiness, longing
i drive to santa monica
i drive to malibu
looking & come home empty handed

the lies i tell me to keep solvent
no bedroom in one split marriage
oh no it is one near the beach
i am sorry i have failed
to have dual & triple minds
what i have learned i have given
what i have in my pocket he has
received
two women have fed him

the dues are not the same
for stealing an apple
as for stealing a car
one gets a slap on the wrist
the other goes to jail
worries, hope against a keeping
positive thoughts permissable

i am jealous of sixteen-year-olds
a middle-aged man says
to take off & have an adventure
initiation into manhood
quitting school, sleeping in a car
in malibu
he is gone & i am sad
& i have not heard from him
i look for him in solitary figures
standing in front of a liquor store
walking beside the highway
leaning on the railing looking out
at the ocean
from a pier
there is longing

3   17   85

a parting

he picks up what the parent
sleeps, works, dreams, dances, fucks, swims.

his crew cut dyed
black; his hair mohawked from a very short crew cut.

his father sees in slo mo
a tied up man whose face is a foot away from a rattlesnake
its mouth once sewed up now the threads slip away
a coming death.

i don't want you near me
get out of my house!
you told me to come here & help care for the boy.

the mother sleeps on a sofa bed
the boy has taken over the bedroom, cassettes, books, half
circle around the foot of his bed, surfing photos on the walls,
clothes disarray in the closet.
he sewed up death.

he had three skateboards
gone within two years, stolen he said. a bike gone last week.
she encouraged hair changes
as for the boy, get out of the way, my heart tears
the boy stitches the hidden
he did not go to the father when he left the mother he went away
with an older boy of another race.

how to avoid the bad
bad drugs bad tv bad discipline bad poorness bad split family
bad collective bad survival bad ownership bad warmth bad love.

surfboards 3
in a corner of his bedroom; beach child.

3   20   85

even similar

god is in our hair, god
is in our arms
thirty years ago, sitting in the overland cafe in sidney,
nebraska, drinking coffee in the greyhound bus station
discussing the existence & non-existence of god
a memory as barry & i get out of his chevrolet & walk toward
the santa monica place
we drink coffee & look at the fountain
butterflies above us
"they write graffitti on our fucking artifacts
artifact on artifact, layer on layer,
who did you take this land from
i'm taking it from you
we put our artifacts on top of their artifacts"
from the new mall we walk to the old mall
we stand at the edge of the bluff
he lights a cigarette
i light a roach & we stare at the ocean & the pier & the string
of lights "the night air surrounds us!"
"& why not drive"
even people with similar tastes are separated by long distances
let him go, letting go, let him fall, let him pick himself up.
let him bail himself out, let him have his own way, let him get
a job, let him get out of the house
in order to be big you have to work little
a thought about film acting &
all the technological changes we have experienced
we live in a very confused time: time pursues
let the tv take us away, let drugs do the work

unfortunately god
god is the best we can be
god is not separate from evil god is the struggle to give reason

a choice of desiring & choosing good over evil
free will is simply dying to be born
making a living without hurting without killing with mutual respect
allowing each connection a free valued deliberate learning

and we share the lights on fountain a desolate street
waiting to go home
as i left a friend on pacific after a long bus ride from the other
side of the city he said "we are all such poor creatures"
the time passed quickly as i was talking with him & i was not
conscious of the cities we were passing through

god is in the news we bring to heaven

3   27   85

seriously mistaken

seriously mistaken, spoken
about an opponent branding
its opposite view
is a face simple, flint open

a teacher has to be smart
to stay
it takes a wounding
to get the sweet vulnerability

the love of two men in a car
late night talking desolate fountain
an extrovert & an artist
coffee & cookie & talk of god
butterflies above the fountain

terror of a jungle blade
city face smooth as commerce
the true commerce is mercy
healing from an assumed melancholy

the priest where he was given water
in what acre in what long hot row
the union of a literary friendship
a woman teacher helping a male
student learn

has a whiteness as rain
tipped & open & fell
to see beauty is to see distance
brother of learning & sister

spiritual
when all is done & gone we gave
we cleaned & so much of life is
whether was was glorious, wrath

was not in the beginning line
tragedy & the river thine
she stood in the bedroom doorway
looking where the hunt was

it has a fountain & it has dryness
stepping into the bath
i saw for all the returning
the realness of the nakedness

all in a fleeting dinner
to celebrate an order of sunlight
morning bath open window
the boy returned & the father had
felt heartache & was now relieved

3   31   85

we are all such poor creatures

i look back at the inclusion
meaning understanding loyalty
worship learning invocation
gods ladies wheat fields old
cars
we fall asleep without saying
i love you after a goodnight
kiss
wanting the external cleaned
up
task before cleaning a worship
-ful soul
my son with his mother & woman
with me & i
have to meet with a counselor
chosen by the santa monica
police department to mend
a running away to punk caves
malibu
some crazy drugs involved there
the bedding warm now
found a terror & a togetherness
when i left our home of eleven
years west hollywood
cows don't steal
one can not run away from within
to keep out that which is harsh
i am going to have to tell him
what to do
the incidents are minor: skate-
boarding on the old mall; drink-
ing a can of colt 45 in public
parking lot behind the 321 club

trying to understand the poverty
splitting
he is no longer baby dylan
he wants to make up his own mind
about things
knife cuttings into an old tree
in front of our house it is me
the terror draws long horizontal
incisions & the freshly marked
crazy & husky cut in front of me
twice a few days ago
my son too experiences the chang-
ing set-up for unidentified
badness a group of teenagers
hanging out nothing to do
i include the terror within my
work & i paint over the gang names
with whiteness & i carry away the
leaves boat shaped to take me away

4   4   85

memorial day 1985

the cat caught a small bird
brought it into the kitchen
took it under the table into
the corner the cat's favorite
spot for death & shit

jacaranda bloom against the
far dwelling
its mirrored lavender fall
a painting that i live by

to give to what is known
there will be no allowances
bodies in the bay bodies in
the rivers

my son has gotten back into
surfing he has left the old
mall where he got into trouble
where he was watched followed
wanting to be mistaken
i am glad he has gotten back
into the water

wedding voices late gifts joy
old acting friend with gracious
strength a relaxed opening
my son now lives with his
mother visits me &woman
once a week
he has given up shuttling

leaves have fallen again
loss but hope for happiness

the boy lives with his mother
spends much time with girl
who lives with her mother
death to a way of living of
sharing boy has ended

the cat made a deep guttural
growl when i tried to take
the bird from its mouth
"he's not going to let you
get it" the day the hunter
moved fast through the house
each time after it entered

5   26   85

the youth then

youth set a wheat field on fire
youth ransacked a country school
youth dreamed listened to ricky nelson i'm walkin'
fats domino in the winter wheat nebraska summer
stole dreamed wanted desperately to prove his
manhood torn from loneliness practiced baseball
morning after morning
it is hot & there is guilt for not being everyall
born to serve anguish humility love desperate beauty

down to nothing & he steals he studies he goes
to school at a country red schoolhouse two stories
two miles from the sioux ordnance dept
he lived in the housing project called ordville
surrounded by fields of wheat & dirt roads farms
fences small towns
the stakes have gone up in the big west coast city
is it because youth can be/has been murdering brutally
occasionally on the wide well protected rich homes
went in & killed the whole family
or fires set in loneliness
anger split sexual &aggressive& denies consequence
its love now & he's okay
he meets her she drives
pretty happy it is nice to see there is anger in
adolescence
for fields barren seemingly youth runs his car over
dormant winter
for the hunting to sell to buy pepsi's french fries
wings love lost the custom of becoming ones environment
the youth then down the silver colored fire escape
soccer in the school yard
blood forehead shin trash ragged cut
to grow up with the guns going off the constant weekly daily

exploding bombs ammunition from the second world war
o well i am in los angeles now & i drive the speed limit &
most pass even the thirty five under the three freeways
heading onto the hollywood freeway
to get home & be safe & think about my sixteen & a half year
old boy he is happy now although the school year was rough
on him his best friend growing up got sent to reform school
& i was terribly saddened
he was an excellent drawer & a great quarterback he was quietly
strong
all the bad things i did growing up & i got away with some got
caught with several but was always given another chance had fines
to pay
fatherless boys looking for that strong male authority to stop them

7   4   85

the bed i rest on & a book by kazin

its brown cool cover, its red & black light
love poem window rest; she has gone to withdraw money
food the son has gone to the beach on a bus
theres jazz, croissants, coffee, new boxer shorts
for the boy.

theres a love-seat that pulls into a bed
he watches tv in it late night cat seeking cool air
movement from the square fan, ritz, coke, berries.
i wonder will he be there the appointed time
he has been most times, his joy, his struggle
he wore them this morning & they fit.

red roses on the brown dining table, prayers love
she sleeps naked, fan on, rest needed
the young female cat sleeps next to her typewriter
stains, bus ocean hot night reaching a youth
young girl on bank of river, friendly, farm-like
i met my son as i stepped off the number 4 bus
he was standing in front of the 321 club
do you want to meet my girl; he took me to meet her
mall, three girls, by a phone.

its openness, its pillow, its clean memory
he the man past has used terms: alienation, loss,
need, anxiety, ;he has also said: love, joy,
childhood, work, help, respect, union unity.

for it is seen in the boy & it is seen in the woman
hope, youth, restore, there was a feeling of friend
i went to the stadium to buy tickets; the boy went
to the beach with friends; she went to the bank
& she went to the grocery store & she got the car
washed. earlier she had cleaned up outside.

leaves, watered
we watch baseball at the stadium, on tv
five months we have been living together
both of us grew up in nebraska
we share as much as we can & we fall back & rest
i place the fan in her direction, turn off lights
take my book into another room.
she rests after working hard in the morning
for it is hope that has given time to be thankful
for all the arisings heat passion desire doubt
the killing death exalts curious time, refolds.

7   11   85

there are moments of sheer brilliant love

there are moments of sheer brilliant love
when the love making is good & the consideration for another
makes all bad thoughts fade
even time is suspended like in a good story well told
for to keep feeling like a bird sensitive to external winds
walkings by phonings
the loss for me is always to be no longer connected to words
to work to love & harmony being boundary enough for gods
                                        protected
seem to flourish its dead discursiveness

the love making was good & the jazz that preceeded it also
a sensual cleanliness
the excitement of being out in the city rich with its exotic
wildness
the card of flowers she gave me
its elusive appetite an understanding there are fields dreams
that i stand no nearer to than on the other side of a closed door
the food attractive & fresh & wholesome its firmness its tenderness

the brown train goes under a green underpass gray smoke
blue train gray smoke white sky

when there is no need to transcend her body
for the coldness & the clean & the white
the heart shaped moon desire a listening to what pulls on the inner
lucidity
making love is for me a green pleasure
the last word eve says in *paradise lost* is "restore"
the food she cooks & the places & times she cleans
to restore love to gold to hold its honor even among similes its
thieves like a night
renters wholesalers designs configurations oval departures trees
beaks stories wants all changed unto a commited honor

to moderate a seeking
wherein boy where woman a man serves in order to achieve an
equal
for the hidings seem to be killed a constant
there are moments of sheer brilliant love
her skirts black her skirts gray
blue & pink she has in her hand

it is in a home where there is love
& if simplicity in home & two & three
a woman place for the man for the boy

the flowers she gave to me were dragged from me
in order to clear time for the life
for there is time for happiness & this is such a time
there is love & there is also damage
we have been all our dreams a waking
she has the understanding love itself is a happy he understands
he has also hurt her & he loves her for hope restores

8   18   85

east hollywood meditation
8-20-87
to
12-23-88

violet crimson

there is a violet crimson flower
that is ann stanford. ann stanford
is one of america's best poets.
she studied verse with yvor winters.
she went to him once & asked him
about writing poetry & he told her,
"simplicity."

she goes back to anne bradstreet
in terms of cold morning lucidity:
thrift, hard work, restraint, religious
compassion. she added an individual
classicism, doubt, but retained mystery.

she translated *the bhagavad gita* into
verse like she said the original was
in. she learned sanskrit in order
to translate it. her own style
seemed to change after that work.
love & duty.

there is a violet streak in love.

8   20   87

the swordfish was good last night

like she said, '50s cooking, fried,
filet of sole, slightly breaded swordfish
good french fries & cole slaw, long-necked
bottle of beer; it was my 47th birthday,
working on my 27th film, in 1987, a lot
of sevens.

corn, far as the eye can see, all the way
to the horizon, green, moist land, hilly,
many stacks of hay, brown.   eastern kansas.
there is much history in that state.

a negative of a photo that shows me
playing the "governor" in "kansas," a
dark navy blue suit, white shirt, with red
predominant in the tie, blue & white stripes
the governor stands in front of an american
flag, has his picture taken.

saturday leave, work monday, tuesday, wednesday
fly back thursday, my son & i
he has never been on location before except
when he was a baby up in san francisco & vacaville
shooting "the all-american boy."

speech-making, televsion interviews, parades
years ago, i kept seeing the number 47 in my
mind; so far, it has been genuine, fun, work,
money, travel, loyalty, co-operation, harmony,
intimacy, t-shirts bought, many good meals, one
light & excellent one.

the writing endures the waiting, rejections, dis-
loyalties, hurts, personal failures, wants,
forgives with work, opportunity, resurrected love.

9   3   87

why poets picket the l.a. times

when i went to sleep
i saw sunflowers sunflowers
roads & dreams of them

i am sorry i dont have any bright ideas to please you
thats okay, the eight year old girl said, you dont have to
thats what women are supposed to do

charlie parker is buried in kansas city
you know what motel is spelled backwards
letem

rain & lightning
that was the first vision i saw
falling asleep
in kansas
the last night i was in kansas shooting a movie entitled
"kansas"

the day my son & i got home
she met us across the street at the taxi
we saw two cops & a plain clothes cop standing near
talking
we saw them carefully move up to a nearby house
we went into our home with suitcases backpack skateboard
i looked through the window a few minutes later & saw
a heavy armenian drug dealer handcuffed
we went outside to watch
& i said thats the third time we watched this
justice triumphs the plain clothes man said
opening his door
getting in next to the dark armenian drug dealer
he looked straight out at us

the state flower
windy along the sides of roads
among greenery & moist
land where i returned to with my son while i was playing
the governor of kansas in a movie entitled "kansas"
shooting in lawrence

the night earlier the producer had cooked pasta with a
light tomato sauce we had gone to the eldridge bar
talked with other actors director cinematographer editor
producer manager movie star
i said thank you to george litto he said lastly after
appreciations i love you & i said i love you
the second film i acted in for him
i met allen ginsberg in the park inn motel later i
introduced my son dylan to him
he was leading joy i was fortunate to be working
when i went to sleep i saw sunflowers

9   10   87

a hope for love, work

there must be hope, a light one
can see. there must be a light,
even among the hopelessness. other-
wise, the building is for naught. a
hope of opportunity, a hope of
creativity, of communication,
communion. a hope for love, work.
fellowship, community. a light one
can see in the words. the particular
from the general. a falling down
to the ground. where the crown is.

9   21   87

november friday

in this room with four lights on
the breakings begin, a crying its fear
a failure to sit among madness
damaged cassettes, no word from rare mystery

"i had an emotional outburst
at the evening, saying essentially
that we are all sick, not just our kids
who get into trouble, who have trouble
with school"
"you identify with your son
& he identifies with you, did you hear
what i said, he identifies with you"

i get so crazy & i think i will never work
again, & anxiety walks to the end
of the food line on skid row, begins its wait
again
"what a doomy feeling about life"
for thine is the mystery unrevealed
a hardness, an unexplained terror

the god damn lights herald an open ness
i go crazy over minorities who are not
gracious to me, wanting forever acceptances

i have not cried yet for her death
i cried when i wrote poems of love & humility
fourteen & ten years before she died
& i denounce those who will not reveal more
more change & more death

the overlays suffocate me, i throw them about
away from the frontier

which is a kneeling unto solace, a bewildering
open ness used among loss a dream unannounced

i parked by the orange trees & i walked through
the halls, & fear was harsh, alone but for her
gracious teaching, a light for her words on the
page, spiritual visiting

11   13   87

freedom

i give a half naked artist ten small boxes
of rice krispies; he rides with me to the post office

rice food; leave the rice, take the chicken in curry,
green vegetables

i cover the money with church; read the work of minors
& majors

inner experience boned; the first is the highest

over all the market is next; what poetry does to time
& the imagination

the real split nausea despair an acute avoiding the real
pain how ordinary body breathes a trust implicit in gift
one true real birth

shut the outer shut the attempts at overlay; those who
have no real beginning

nurturing dream reflection, a work near one's home;
sunflowers alongside highways entered, carried moisture
greenness

she put precision in a class, a whole & a half; one woman
loved man, woman, child, she is first to me

in terms of continuity there are many splits, contemporary
that have been dead for years

to cooperate means innocence itself hope, a second metaphor

to be holy alone, a solace searched for; our society has
been separated from the words by visuals more captivating

plural politics, merchants for their door; i am not going
to the frontier, i am going to the window

for i can offer only the branches, squares & shadows, for
without running

it is the hope she pointed to, family & classical knowledge,
strictness, simplicity, an intimate relationship with her
words

wanting things to move faster in front of him; the mother
then dies & the family disintegrates; i cover the money with
earth

11   16   87

Giving Thanks To A Teacher
Recently Deceased

Ann Stanford died on July 12, 1987 of liver cancer. She was born in La Habra on November 25, 1916. I told her son at the Forest Lawn Memorial, "She was a wonderful teacher." He replied, "She was a wonderful mother."

To me, a 33 year old poet who was studying with her in 1973, she was a rare human in a cold, rational college in Northridge. She treated each person in the class with equal fairness. I studied verse with her one semester & the following one, structural grammar. She looked up from her book when she was reading & stopped & said, "Let's enjoy the journey & not worry so much about the end." After many students had kept asking her about what questions might be on the structural grammar mid-term exam.

To inspire is the purpose of poetry. She was an inspiration. In the year I studied with her, I wrote three books of poetry, each of which has been published. I loved, I love her poetry. Her poetry is the real inspiration; she was the human worker. She studied poetry with Yvor Winters at Stanford. She went to him once & asked him how to approach poetry & he replied, "Simplicity." Her poetry was very strict. It loosened up at times. There seemed to be a change after she learned Sanskrit & translated *The Bhagavad Gita.*

Her poetry has a sense of compassion, love, continuity, religion & doubt. It is evident that she cares deeply for her family. She is dead and I have gone to two memorials & I am not satisfied & I want to stand on a Los Angeles corner & read out loud from all of her poetry books. She goes back to the Puritans. She goes back to the earth.

11   16   87

a test of character

i give thanks to philip whalen
for writing "For C."   its last line
"At least I broke and stole that branch with love."
many times the woman i love
& i have quoted that line, & other poets also.

11   20   87

the question is

what am i comfortable with?

i make my living as an actor
acting & poetry, blood, love.

she said you attack women
he said fuck you, you are
full of shit.

son, woman, grass
che said when they give into
your demands
the revolution is over.

i asked a woman psychologist
when you speed read
do you find pleasure in reading

in poetry you have to read
each word; i read slow, i find
pleasure in reading.

i am comfortable with emotion
it takes me away from thought

to be possessed by mystery.
with intelligent & pleasureable
writing, clean lucidity.

i am comfortable with revolution
in poetry, to gain more entrance

first a revolution wants an arm
then it wants the body; i speak
of balance & clarity not gender.

                    11   30   87

its an old poem

its an old poem
i return to in poetry
& the shoes are worn
but solid
;she has loneliness
she regained mystery

11   30   87

december in los angeles

the bus ran three red lights
crisp cold day
strong wind light rain

my son gets a try out
thursday at noon, thrifty's

i got money for a tree &
a honey baked ham
two pies from house of pies

prayer for obedience nightly

12   16   1987

like the road it beckons its pearl dead

i live in a library of movies on z
football & basketball on 2 4 7 9 11
god the pain my son i worry
my life he's my life my boy my blood
last night i watched two movies on z

i came to this town to be an individual star
a man who takes things into his own hands
fighting the institution the bad guy the enemy
someone coming at him from behind a set up
then i just wanted to act to make my living
as an actor
i love movies i love the woman i live with
she buys flowers she buys groceries
she has a career as a writer as a teacher
she keeps a journal she writes novels
poetry she writes she studies she reads
she sustains me she sustains me

i live in the literary world i live in
the acting world whenever i am fortunate enough
to work i recently worked on "kansas" the governor
time goes i don't go out for auditions
i take walks i read poetry i watch movies on tv
i talk to friends on the phone
to be always the honest man

i live in a library of lights
it gets harder to live among the words
proustian my lights movies like books used to be

1   3   1988

wisdom is the power breath gives to trees

& all living things; each dwells in an infrastructure so
long as the webs do not permit entrance to drive in & out
of; so each dwells in a house bought

1   16   88

4 lights on

4 lights on
the tan cowboy boots off
next to a bookcase of
manuscripts, clippings, letters

the quiet human voice
there is a need for it

i drove the 20 miles
knocked on his door
got him to his appointment on time

he has taken down all his punk pictures
now he has surfing photos, family photos
nearly naked women pictures, a painting
by his mom, a rectangular mirror, neat
everything is neat on the walls

he looks good
hes happy working, surfing, going up &
down the coast
his friend rudy has a car
they drove to oxnard last week, no waves
they came back to santa monica & found
good waves

an empty father
like a boy leaving home
he wants to live in one place
hes tired of traveling back & forth
all the time

vans, alarm clock, lamp, desk
the main two first, he & his soul
i pray for him to god every night

he talks about going on a 3 day surfing trip
with rudy & scott
he wants to learn how to ski
he opened a bank account
he gives his mother money every week

2   22   88

february in california

the out of work actor
had a conversation with a limousine driver
whats the biggest trout you ever saw?

he got home she bathed
he was watching how beautiful james mason was
"odd man out"
she came in
"are you deeply invested in watching that movie?"
the inconsistencies drive me mad

he cleaned up he came back into the bedroom
he sucked her left nipple she stroked his cock
they kissed the beauty went on they made love
an hour before noon

he closed his eyes
he saw two people
on a moderately sized wagon pulled by horses
through a country side
in the back of the wagon
a larger than life candle lit

then a wagon of red roses
evidently the guy with the trout stepped into
his single in west hollywood
the out of work actor was in a hurry
we must come to each other
like in the bible
in humility & brokenness

he rages & she rages in his desperate furie
furie for politics furie for luck furie for
bewilderment furie recognition gone wanting

he stays inside & watches tv tv tv movies sports
news he one day out of desperation sits down &
reads out loud the marriage of heaven & hell by
blake even that then is not understood the way
it was twenty years ago what was death & what
was life

the out of work actor has to get over his fear
concerning when will he ever work again

the last thing he saw
was a wagon of peach colored roses

2   26   88

there is rain in the california day

the woman i love & i
went over to a friend's apartment
in the los feliz area

we drank red wine & ate a delicious dinner
the woman i love had brought orchids
& a chocolate cake from trader joe's

the women discussed love myths
exuberant devotion to language

we watched "over the edge" on her vcr
the woman i love said on the way home
"i like her because she's optimistic;
i hadn't realized how much i had missed that."

2   29   88

the story is

the story is
he smokes thai weed
lays in bed
watching tv
he would say
movies on tv
& sports
& news

he wants
to discover
a new way
in poetry

his mind
is full
of ads

he forgets
most

through
his mind
like
newspaper

he analyzes
the candidates
in primaries
he dislikes
narrative

the story is
image free
market

4   16   88

one of my favorite groups was savoy brown

the first night i arrived in los angeles
i got a job as a waiter at the old world restaurant
worked there for two years
the longest i ever worked at a job except for 3 years navy
then i got my first good paying acting job: 2 months
in the film "the all-american boy"
written & directed by charles eastman, starring jon voight
i played parker, a small town friend photographer
i made me enough money to last a year for my wife & son &
me

college for several years, verse with ann stanford
ten months driving a cab for santa monica red top
played the port & was good & fast & lucky

my son is now nineteen; i have lived in santa monica 6
years, west hollywood 11 years, east hollywood 3 years

to go back & to name, to think i have named before
it deadens me, instead there are black & white shoes 13
years old

twenty years in this town, a movie coming out this summer
i bought a pair of tan cotton pants at ross, 15 bucks, a
silk tie for 5

the particulars i dream at waking
a young woman opens the door comes in says someone
chases her
a man goes to the door locks it
at the moment of locking he turns yells out twice mother

he mirrors manifest destiny he mirrors mountain
he keeps what is broken for a wildness

the first night in los angeles i went to the strip
cyrano's, the old world i got a job took a month before i
got to working regularly

my first job in new york was at quicksilver messenger service
41st off fifth
i studied acting in new york with frank corsaro

music points its finger upward, the music is gone, you
remember it, therefore it's ancestry

may 14   1988

look, i write about the movies

i was up in san francisco working on a movie
playing a chauffeur for a rock star
i would eat at a little cafe near a park in north beach

the night before this particular breakfast
was the academy awards on tv
a balding, middle-age man dressed in a suit
& carrying a briefcase
sat with a younger, intelligent-looking man
he also had a briefcase
they sat down next to me
"did you see the awards last night?   weren't they dreadful?
& that gown meryl streep was wearing was awful..."

they went on & trashed the awards
& toward the end of that run, the older man kept repeating
"well, you know what my mother used to say:
the theatre is not made up of ladies & gentlemen

the theatre is not made up of ladies & gentlemen."

after they finished their meals, had more coffee served,
they each reached into their briefcases & pulled out a
script they were working on, & began talking about content
& how they might sell it to the movies

5   15   88

10

i am happy that dylan is working
cafe cafe, santa monica place
he began working there on may 10th

television dominates my life
basketball playoffs, news, movies
music

holly went to the library
annie called & invited us to eat
at a thai restaurant saturday night
near her house
"oh annie you re too generous"
"no i'm not"
"annie you re too generous"

terrifyingly lost in love making
holly's legs were so pretty &
she was so clean
wearing just a pair of white panties
when she first joined me in bed
i was watching joseph campbell on myth
after he finished, we began our
love making ritual, one of

sunday night at the ash grove
highland & santa monica blvd
michael c ford, holly prado, me,
william claxton, produced by harvey
kubernik, poster by heather harris
ed pearl proprietor
should be fun

monday i file for a new unemployment
claim, should get it
from working on "kansas" last year

tuesday i meet with a lawyer
to begin filling out forms for divorce

i write in our bedroom
poetry books & myths & biographies

my eyes have gone to tv
somehow i must learn how to shed the
visual attraction

best & live athletes
i played basketball in the rain & snow
& warmth of gyms
remember when glass backboards came in

june   3   1988

humility

humility
thats what we re learning

tv is watched mucho
by actors who would prefer
to be working

an actor goes up
to a penthouse on sunset
meets a director of a film
has a good fifteen minute talk
with him about texas
where both were born
acting school in new york
mutual friends among actors
the actor comes home happy
two hours later he is empty
goes a little nuts

he watches movies on tv
reads the paper has coffee
at farmers market

handcuffs
he fears being in prison

his son works lives
with his mother
the father has to accept loss
he is happy the son works
espresso cafe in the mall

he reads his old poems
a poem about an actors' strike

eight years ago
a poem about praise a range
of loss tough & claw

tomorrow a fellow poet & wife
n w corner of vermont & fountain
baseball game dodger stadium
so empty & so full of humility
praise tv praise hollywood praise
a sharing of talk about poetry
today in the market

6   16   88

east hollywood meditation

my father, after his retirement
from the civil service for
health reasons, would get up early
& go downtown to a bar
drink a few beers, buy a newspaper
come home
sometimes in the summer, mid morning
i found him half asleep at the
kitchen table, a half drunk glass
of beer in front of him

that was thirty years ago
& now my son at age nineteen
has given up spending half his time
here
& now my son lives full time
with his mother in santa monica
near his job at the santa monica place

my son has gone from me & i miss him
& the loss is a hell & i return
to that which has given me birth
the movies
when i first went to new york
to study acting
i went to hundreds of plays, movies
times square at 2 a m or broadway
& 47th area at 10 a m
movies from which i have made a living
for fifteen years, & some others part
time
now i watch movie after movie on tv
movies by bunuel & preminger & ford
true, there is a writers' strike on

17th week
true, i love to be taken away
as a child i read novels novels &bios

my father would sit & read pocket books
westerns, detective stories, & work
crossword puzzles
he read all his life
he had a sixth grade education
my mother eighth grade

i return to my birth & i lose myself
in external stories & moving images
movies are about heroes
made bright with light

june 29   1988

quest

thats what it is for me
its a search for the son
metaphor through the city
santa monica west hollywood
east hollywood
through songs of religion
songs of the city our
mother of city ocean building
up after tearing down
a deconstructuralist's corner
gas station empty lot mini
mart
through broken law through
the book of job the poems
of baudelaire "i hate nature"
its a search for my son
through teaching him to read
to print to handwriting
he wore glasses at age five
he began surfing earlier
among the sagas of fathers
this is a son for my son
gone & free & working & living
in one place with his mother
for the first permanent time
in fourteen years
always before shuttling
west hollywood to santa monica
santa monica to west hollywood
to east hollywood &constant
it is a quest through the city
born of metaphor of woman
the father a constant reason

to retrieve the badness
to pray every night
for a year
he got a job & it is almost
two months
he has worked & been happy
he is gone from me but i find
solace & happiness in his work
helping pay the rent at home
a settling goodness a hope

june 29, 1988

july in los angeles

the cops are out
catching people driving drunk
under the influence
out on holidays nights

the people seem most
interested in reading
block busters
satires & info

rarely do people smoke
weed at dinner parties
private gatherings

the sounds of cars crashing
at intersections is familiar
work & entertainment &food

europeans love los angeles
because los angeles is the
center of nothingness

everyone is in a hurry
to get home & eat their
hamburgers

"we've had our swingerburgers
& coffee coolers at the old
world" on sunset

the search for the old &
the new in the media
whats good what has
character &enduring

there is a placing of limits
eating lobster & corn on the
cob & drinking beer in san pedro
cool night among mexicans portuguese

a straight quick shot almost
from east hollywood diagonal

a new breed gets high & rides
the bus for movements sakes
the humanity & the absurd

7   27   88

los angeles night

i masturbated in front of the tv
with the curtains drawn
only the tv light on
i was watching late night tv & i
masturbated & i heard people
walk by & i tried to hide my cock
with my cotton robe
& now when i get up late at night
when i can not sleep &
almost immediately after
she gets up & goes to the bathroom
i wonder did the people walking by
see me & tell her they saw me
masturbating in front of the tv

7   27   88

boy voice

it made me feel good
my son called said
his friend & mother
liked me in
"over the edge"

he was also happy
looking forward
to next tuesday
when i am taking
he & his friend
to a baseball game

i have missed him deeply
since he began living
full-time with his mother
he works near there
but i am happy
he is working
likes his job
helps out at home
has a kitty
"little jake"
3 month old female

"i love you" he said
"i love you" i said

7   27   88

hollywood elegy 2

i found a dime
& i saw your face
a stalled van
doors open
no one there
two chp officers
investigating
in the midst
of a downtown
freeway
interchange
i heard
the radio say
raymond carver
poet
short story writer
port angeles washington
dead

8   5   88

feminine

i remove the crystal
from the lines
she steps back in image
feminine
& forward feminine
with shields
5 times in shifting light
then she turns profile
her hands upraised
her head upward
a shining light silver

she seems to walk away
in the same spot
her back toward me
delicate full
a small waist

she dances upward
turning three quarters left
her head over her left shoulder
its three sails
her hand over birth
a ship a woman breasts light
past her in the furthest room
a rectangle of light reflected
light bulb under an arch

8 5 88

dear . . . .

dear . . . .
it was lovely making love with you tuesday night late
after you taught
august 9th roses
hot pink
they opened up the next day
your body was cold & clean & curvy
it was as if the ritual made it more than the first time
yet the first time also

8   11   88

collect my thoughts

i waited for august fifth
the day "kansas" was supposed to open
i waited for august fifth
hoping that i would get hired for "night game"
i waited for august twelfth
i waited for september twenty-third
i waited for

sadness in waiting
a tree seen through bars bamboo
anguish exhilaration
that night in durango it felt like rats
were running across my chest
the heart of my mother
was rare & like a dove
waiting for death
after my father died
she lost her will to live
she died two years later

it felt like rain
i could see east high from the porch bedroom
city swans & bluebirds & aladdin
a walk that is shaded by memory
in a city at the foot of the mountains
trains & rocks & mountain streams
driving across the sagebrush sunset
a general store & all the family
came to live with
he lost his spirit when he lost his store
he joined the civil service in the thirties
it felt like grain
to be walking in city park looking
at the polar bears the soft ball games

i went back into my homeland to do "kansas"
i won many "i speak for democracy"contests
when i was in high school
i played the governor of kansas in the movie "kansas"
my father & my mother i am almost fifty
twenty-five years ago i left sidney nebraska
to pursue acting in new york city
i sit in east hollywood waiting for a movie
i acted in last august september to come out
i also think of my loving family
the harshness & the gentleness of the plains

8   12   88

to be a poet in hollywood is to be alone

i thought as i was walking west along sunset over the
hollywood freeway
i remember years ago when i was living in west hollywood
doing drugs day & night
an actor friend called & asked if he could come over &
get high
i said yes
i was reading *the collected poems of allen ginsberg*
when he arrived
when he knocked i placed the book open to my spot on top
of the console tv in the middle of the living room
against the wall
he came in we smoked some weed & talked for half an hour
when he left he walked past the opened ginsberg book
& said in a low voice to me "you fag lover"
dialogue communication charisma physical beauty is the
order of the day in hollywood
it is difficult to be a poet in hollywood because the word
is not the profit
to be alone is to be alone with a few rare poets who actually
read & write poetry study it quote it learn how to shape &
how to understand its devotional aspect
there is poetry its movement & colors depth character inner
concerns film knowledge in "mean streets" in the great film
"citizen kane" each image adds to the whole vision
there is actually a page of poetry on the screen in d.w.
griffith's "broken blossoms"
when my book *the jon voight poems* was published i gave a
reading marty scorsese came he gave me an acting job in his
next film after the reading
there is poetry in michael curtiz & raoul walsh
but i am talking about what the poet carries around within
hollywood is the land of movies make believe fun escape
the big dreams the commonwealth of all the projection of light

the windows that i look at are books: books by blake plath
sexton pound olson whitman *the bible* freud plato bullfinch
homer virgil chaucer lorca dorn barnes milton
the big dreams move me with words & film
i remember unfinished the hope heart communication mind bone
i remember the businesses along the street the bars with
exotic dancers the supermarkets liquor stores flower &wedding
boutiques many different ethnic restaurants clothing stores
businesses buildings come & are replaced torn down & new
writing on the walls by invisible hunger to be recorded
recorded on a wall that is being torn down
the whole side of my heart was a tree
i remember seeing a tree through the bamboo & the bars
a bow shaped like a boat &

8   24   89

september

there is light, a bath
the body wonderful

i watch the olympics
nothing coheres
or makes any sense to me

it is a passive life
it felt like insanity
last night

sense, herbs, female &
male fights male
the book reviews
& the nausea lips
stacks of cassettes
in front of books

my son has a bright face
clean teeth shiny eyes
strong arms from surfing
two, three times a day

worry beads & a silver
drinking cup
in front of books
the television at the end
of the bed

bed, bath, rain, highway
i remember when i was little
thinking about roads, just
all the many roads, curves

for i read it until
it devours me

9   18   88

collision on fountain & mariposa

many dark races standing on the southeast corner
fountain & mariposa
staring at a man trapped upside down in his overturned
car
"you're lucky you're okay," said the paramedic to the man
after he had been helped out by the firemen
there have been many wrecks on this corner
over the years
& many at the intersection of normandie & fountain

we live three houses south of fountain
on the east side of mariposa
we hear the wrecks & run out to see what happened

11   23   88

the painter

they have blocked his window
with a parking structure
he can no longer see hollywood boulevard
cutting diagonally toward vermont
nor the hollywood sign nor car billboards
nor the observatory

he has nailed brecht joyce pound burroughs
tapies to the wall
has made sculptures assemblages with bottles
empty of whiskey & water
nailed workboots to the wood

he made a brown sculpture one foot high
with holes for a hand & wrote
i live in filth i love filth
his dark paint drips from nuances

things only another painter would notice
the small tears in the canvas
paint drips
the off colors

the bottoms & sides of his feet are covered
with dark paints
he wears sandals
he goes out to cafes rides the buses
tells me about incidents with fellow passengers
that confront him
he "postured" me
so i "postured" him back ("i adjusted my jacket")

he has an art show opening this coming sunday

& he reads me poems that he is going to read
poems about living in a board & care home
poems about confrontations in sunset cafes
poems about his imagination about his sister
poems about friendship

"it's about money," he said, & "i'm dangerous."

11   23   88

theres dust on the tv

theres dust on the tv
theres dust in the eye of eternity

12   7   88

they write it down

i told her the three phrases
i had been thinking about recently
were
glamour gods
border woman
gypsy scholar
the next day she called asked me
what were those phrases you told me

the woman i love
the woman i live with
wrote down in our bedside journal
i love your poem "humility"

i bought swordfish for two &
a new york steak for my son
string beans & new potatoes
i'll buy a chocolate creme pie
from the house of pies tomorrow

i took my son to see "rain man"
shared french fries & hot chocolate afterwards
i drove carefully on the freeway coming home
heavy rain

books baseball gloves many cowboy shirts
christmas music on the radio
a warm, modest christmas

we took a five day vacation
went to santa barbara
pismo beach ,visited a friend & his new wife
in morro bay

i see the phrases, & i see them newly

12   23   88

HUMILITIES
2-1-89
to
6-20-90

remember

remember my mother
she rode in a rumble seat
on her way to amarillo
while she was pregnant
with me

remember my brother
closest in age to me
he helped me
many times
with money & reason

remember my friend
he ran lines with me
sparked ideas
helped me in
emergencies

remember love &desire
the reason i run
after acting jobs
poems

remember rain
its music love fresh

remember my woman
she loved me fed
me held me worked

remember home
nebraska flat hilly
brown &golden wheat

remember my father
he worked hard
for his family
stoic reliable

remember my son
sleeping in the
living room
tv & ocean & kiss
as we leave each destiny

              2   1   89

father son dialogue

"i'm sorry this car is old; i wish that we had a better
one."
"at least we don't have to take a bus.   at least we don't
have to walk."

"de niro may be the best actor."
"yeah, but he's not the best basketball player."

"did you enjoy the grateful dead concert in oakland?"
"yeah, it's a lot more mellow than punk."
"did you go to a concert every night?"
"no, just one night."
"what'd you do the other nights?   where did you sleep?"
"in the truck."
"cold?"
"yeah.   i was glad to get home.   we just walked around
the parking lot."
"lot of people there?"
"yeah, it was jammed.   we just looked at the people; we
saw one couple, punk, he had a long red mohawk & he had
a thing they put on mean dogs, a. . ."
"a muzzle?"
"yeah, & she was leading him like a dog.   she had him on
a harness."

"i ate a lot of falafels, vegetarian ones.   i liked them."

"was it rough there?"
"everything seemed okay, no trouble."

"how many of you went?"
"six.   we all chipped in to rent the truck."
"look, i'm glad you went & i'm glad you had a good time &
i'm real glad you are home safe; but next time tell me

what you're up to, where you are going, who with, for
how long, okay?"
"okay."
"listen, let's get together & go see a movie this tuesday
night, okay?"
"sure, i'd like to see you."
"let's talk on sunday or monday."

2   6   89

night

i am the deadness man
sorrow
i want to live in a polite society
the i the i the goddam fucking i
but yes there is human in the i
person man hunger work love
sadness over bad things i have done
for family for guilt for worry
death
i am the sorrow man
no work
i worked last in november
also the last audition i had

i want to live for myself
& i want to live for god
living for god is for others
woman son friend stranger
good bad nation or less
unless i am occupied
i am nothing but man who sits
man who drinks who listens
who walks who rides who watches
reads loves falls

i want to be real
real busy man real honest man
real open

night man its day
day in cold time sunshine
why poor those friends

for living in strangeness
is enough

i want to be more than a man

2　6　89

poem love

when sometimes
the love you give me
ash blood
drive free home
an inspiring hope
secure in giving
morse code memory
dit dit dit dah
a test tape of rapture
steady communication
afford to disagree
each affords
motion into forest
then free
until density
an elliptical illusion

so we meet again
in paragraphs
sometimes in modern
poetry at the end
of a paragraph
there is a rhyme

morning my face
the cross the
lighted candle
bell with gold
animal comes
to my side
rain gold rain green
to cross the death plane
cuts spirit darkness

material flight
golden little bells
along sides of skis
table words through plants
a waiting game
street palms mission

2   23   89

middle age

a man starts to panic
when he hits late forties
his hair falls out a little
upper &top back bald
the waist size goes up

eddie g., now there was an actor
& paul muni playing capone
but it wasn't really capone
because capone didn't get shot
like muni did in "scarface"
eddie g. was great in "scarlet street"
& dan duryea he was great, consistent
& he was always dan duryea

those old pictures were good
black & white, the clothes they wore
you know what they had that today's
pictures don't?   faces, great
character actors

you know the west coast jazz
is a little more laid back
than east coast jazz

he buys his hamburger at the chalet
asparagus there too
west hollywood talking about brighton
beach, & the seafood restaurant in
sheepshead bay
apartments where the baths were
where love was met, winter sun

he looks at his journeys &
he drives down sunset
driving through time with words
it is the sunlight & the trees
the voices of children "give me"
"i want to be part of a family"

to pray before & praise tradition
he never saw the shift from good to evil
its goods circular & in & dark
darkness behind the whitest teeth
there is a cross & its dragon bites up
out & a train its smoke recedes
is memory & back in time & then across
the horizon, a propeller, out of the teeth

2   27   89

Father Son Dialogue 2

Son: "We've been going to Huntington Beach, Rudy & me. Saturday, I surfed twice. We stayed out three hours at Huntington. It was really, really fun! Sunday, we went three times. First, we went to Huntington. It wasn't that good. Next, we went to Redondo. It was pretty fun. It was huge! I went so many places!"

Father: "I took the bus from West Hollywood to East Hollywood, caught it on Fairfax, north to Hollywood Boulevard, east to Normandie. I sat in the middle in the backseat. There were two drunk Indians, both ex-Marines. Both had tattoos, pony tails, & both wore tank tops. One was sitting to the left of me, also in the back seat; the other sat in the aisle seat right in front of us."

Son: "I stayed away from the crowd. The waves were 2-4 feet & the set waves were 5 feet. It was fun! You can get a ride all the way in."

Father: "The Indian in front saw a white man about thirty reading a book. 'What are you reading?' 'A play by Shakespeare.' 'He's English, right?' The man nodded yes. 'All English men are fags. Are you English?' 'I'm an actor.' 'All actors are fags.' The bus moved east on Hollywood, past La Brea."

Son: "I bought some brand new wheels; they have pictures of guitars, women & pizza on them. I have my own board. Ian gave me some tracks for my birthday. I sanded my board down. It's all wood. I'm going to draw a wave on it & shellac it."

Father: "Slowly, along the boulevard, the seats & aisle filled up with blacks, Asians, Mexicans, Iranians. The Indians were fucking with each other, the one in back kept pulling the other's pony tail. They began insulting blacks, women, Mexicans. They were totally disillusioned & full of hatred. Their deepest disgust was toward blacks & homosexuals."

Son: "There's a lot of people at the beach today. We laid out in the sun. I was tired from all that surfing. I had rides that I could ride all the way into the shore. I'm glad there's no school this week. I'm going to the beach every day."

Father: "There was a young, powerfully-built black man with a big ass who kept being pushed toward the back. He was obviously a homosexual. He was wearing a blue tank top & blue shorts. By the time the bus reached Vine, he was pressed to the back. He now stood, facing forward, his ass was right smack up in front of the Indian's face. What the Indian hated most was right in his face. I thought this is a perfect short story about a dispossessed Indian & discrimination. What a person hates most will eventually be right in his face. I got off the bus at Normandie."

3   20   89

& the friends

i drive to the glendale library
return chekhov's "the three sisters"
read a few essays in current film mags
& i think about the morning with others
how it was courteous & intelligent, casual
but how when i left i felt like we are all strangers
but it comes in on me like a wave
the market is free & people choose
i am bowed & i am humble this poor actor

4   11   89

Armenians Mariposa

The old Armenian Sarkis plants chard, lettuce, flowers in small earth places around his apartment. He's a wonder, his wife, too. They bring us pastries they make, roses. "You work?" he asked me a number of times. Finally, I took him a cassette from Warner Brothers of a film "Over The Edge," that I played the lead in. It had my name & photo on it. "Movies, Tv," I said. "I'm an actor." He doesn't speak much English. I think he knows what I mean. He brings us lemons from the tree in back by the garage. Recently, young Armenian teenagers have torn up his gardens. He asked us for help. He put up a sign against destruction of things he plants with his hands.

This morning, four young Armenian teens were hanging out on our wall by the sidewalk. They have been seen, in the past, pulling & uprooting plants & flowers from our simple garden. In my robe & Wranglers, I went out & talked to them. "Where do you live?" One pointed down the street; one pointed two doors north of us. I told them that we have seen them destroying plants & flowers that Holly had planted & cared for. "She's a teacher & writer; she works in our home. I'm an actor; I read & study scripts here. Will you please not hang around & do bad things to what she has planted. We don't go over to your house & hang out, do we. We respect your home. I know there aren't many playgrounds around here to play. I know that you are young & have a lot of energy. I have a son; I love children. All we ask is that you respect us; we respect you. We don't do anything to hurt you. Please, from my heart, let's just have a little mutual respect between us." "Okay," the biggest one said.

4 24 89

dear friend

may 15, 1989

dear friend, it just seems to me that poetry once taken fruitful devotion it's either highly intelligent, textual, or frivolous. sex, thighs, beautiful hair, head, body. position, job, influence, house, light, gem, precious shining, i got what's yours. an eerie try to convince another to pay heed to one's views. there is a certain futility in that.

what i'm saying is there is a crazy communication gone. certain ones are then inside the court's favor, many outside. the crippled, the outcast, the hungry. hungry for a human heart, the character, standing & falling, obedient only to devotion, like some are justly zen without the soul.

but there is no crime in trying to convince another; the others then that do not agree are those who turn their backs.

to me it's like an animal that can't be quenched. convince hell convince heaven; it is ours to create an earth out of which we build our own heaven, hell, bridegrooms, faltering castles & fences, where has she gone? there is no one then to lead me; it was a sense of order, dignity, math.

please friend, i need a blue arc, a blue line above it parallel to the ground underneath the darkness; but there is no crime, it was all in him what he described outwards: fear, talk of women, where they cannot go, talk by women, talk of menstrual rituals in northern africa, the quiet desperation, a fierce longing for woman camaraderie, newly arrived fast intellect.

i too then have fear inside me like a round large blue circle for the fear captures the desire of vanity & singularliness. so i sat & looked at pictures read the text of a japanese garden its temple order nature silence centre has reading always calmed me, there was a painting to be talked about.

but then i am in the deepest blue dark anguish; i fear for my son getting into trouble, the accumulation, every two years it seems, how to break the pattern, how can he come to an end say enough to the cause without heed of consequences.

so there is a need for poetry to have community, inward, outward there is also a need to somehow help my son obey the law. i break it & pause, the tears. it amazes me, it awes me, it scares, worries me, puzzles me. above & beyond prayers.

east hollywood

Home Safe

I began writing poetry at age 26. At that time, I was living in a 3½ room, 5 floor walk-up on 25th & Tenth in N.Y.C., $53 a month. I was studying Method acting with Frank Corsaro. Two Off-B'way plays & a film that it looked like I was going to act in, fell through. I had so much emotion inside me that had to get out. Poetry.

I believe that I am a working class poet: many of my poems have been about working as an actor in Hollywood. Working in "Mean Streets," "Alice Doesn't Live Here Anymore," "Taxi Driver," "Blue Collar," "Citizens Band," "Over The Edge," among others. Making a living as an actor, a rare thing. A ruthless business. Working with good people: Scorsese, 6 films, 1 TV show; Demme, 4 films, 2 commercials; Kaplan, 3 movies, 1 TV movie. I write about acting in movies, not from a distance, not mythic, but first hand knowledge. Word. Action. Trust. "Once again," Scorsese said to me when I arrived on the set to work on "Taxi Driver."

So, poetry to me is emotion, memory, work, personal. Camaraderie & love of film. What I love most about working in the movies are telling a story & the comaraderie.

I am also interested in the long poem. I believe poetry is rhythms. I have said elsewhere that, to me, morality is man's fidelity to the word, such that should he give his word, it would have meaning. That if I wrote about something, it would come out of personal experience. And there is also the imagination: a white bird picked me up & carried me over the 50' high peristyle at the top of my climb in the hunt for the assassin. A metaphor for transcending the real involvement.

My poetry stems from my upbringing soil: Texas, Nebraska, Idaho, Colorado, Dorothy Marie Monk, George Northup, combines & baseball fields.

It is a quest to tell the truth of my human existence, in terms of love, death, hope.

Aug. 1, 1989
East Hollywood

money in the bank

today, sept. 2, 1989, i am 49 years old.
holly gave me a cassette of "kansas,"
50 dollars, & a watch. jojo told me
about "police squad." i watched an
episide at 11:30 a.m. pretty wacko!
holly is cooking a duck for dinner.

today is details, love, gifts, humor.
my eyes are going, i need bifocals;
i read without my glasses, hold the
book close to my eyes, it affects
my stomach, i read less, watch tv
more. stay indoors more. am more

irritated by small children yelling,
teenagers hanging out in front of
our apartment; the seeing of these
acts drives me crazy, i have to live
more inner, concentrate on the
inside of this east hollywood home.

the junk society, throwaway society,
selling, p.r., drugged, material, aggressive,
insular, "the haves & the have nots."
there is a religious impulse, a good-
hearted voice, love in our society.
there are poets who devote themselves

to the study of poetry. i love
poetry; i love movies. prose is tough.
there is a poetry festival sponsored
by the city of los angeles the week
of oct. 22 - 28. it is the first time

los angeles has done this.   a first!
a poetry celebration!   hurrah!

we are going to barnsdall park at 1 p.m.
to see & hear a free jazz concert.
my son started working thursday.
i got divorced wednesday.

the hollywood freeway was crowded
headed toward downtown.   i am staying
near home.   holly went to sorbonne
to get a birthday cake.   there are
golden leaves behind my head.
49 years old.   i don't work as much

as an actor as i used to.   but i
signed, renewed representation with
my agent.   i love my son; i love
holly.   i love our cat.   i have 8
dollars in the bank.

9   2   89

garlands & muse & wheat

keats hands on the piano keys, playing
hands reaching out from the water, holding
a ledge, rainy night, men in raincoats,
hats, furtive
a light in a window in a house a light
above in the sky
the war is the chapel & it glows
its trees & circling mountains

we went to a free jazz concert in barnsdall
park today; it was fine, pleasant

a yellow pepper & wheat floating down
a shallow stream
a man burning downward
plane into trees
the seed is what exists between man woman
& the image

"he (keats) was the ultimate romantic," she said.
the candle, a pen
the crowned gold was a covered wagon
his altar: all the human pieces fitting
together, the lines of separation

his beautiful lines, "it's as if he's speaking
to me," she said.

9 2 89

Thursday Night East Hollywood

All day long I've been restless.
My agent called, said your start date
on "The Silence Of The Lambs" has been pushed
back till February 10th. Originally, it was
December 11th. A week's work. Shooting in
Pittsburgh. More time to learn about pigeons.
More time to let my sideburns grow. Time
to practice pounding nails.

My son called me at three in the afternoon.
"Could you help me write an essay about freedom?"
"Yes. How many words?" "500," he said.
"There's a lot of money for first, second & third
prizes. It's not due until December."
"Sure," I said. "Why don't you go to the library,
check out a book that has the Bill of Rights in it,
& check out the First Amendment. That talks about
freedom of speech, freedom of press, freedom of
religion, freedom of assembly. Start with that."
We decided to get together on Tuesday & work on it.

the sights

i saw an old woman with a tattoo,
i saw a mexican man sitting next to a pumpkin
with its carved out face
on a porch at dusk in hollywood

these sights have given me pleasure
fascinated me

i saw two cops pull over four mexican men
who looked like gang guys
in a black original 510 datsun on vermont

today i drove to the beach & took a long walk
ate a small piece of hot italian sausage
from a sausage stand on ocean front walk
south of windward
i drove a friend & his wife to the store &
to the venice library

recently i was contracted to do a movie
in december
then my agent called
i don't go to work on this movie until february
the delay put me in limbo

walks, drives, movies, sex, food
these are the things my body craves these days
i do not order my life around others' wants
my harmony is one sought by my body hunger

11   7   89

los angeles poetry 12 2 89

1) whether the personal use & the use of the mythic, through american history, western culture through homer, *the bible*, the outcasts, islands individuals; olson. 2) henry miller, ginsberg, romantic, sexual, honest in the here & now, particular u.s. detail, a nice old tradition here, memory, continuity. t. s. eliot, pound, back through tradition, a cutting away, to dante. church form usurper cage fertile study devotion. eliot carried dante in his coat pocket, pound liked the troubadours, he said "i will know more about poetry than anyone in the world, by the time i'm thirty"; pound said showed in *the cantos* that language is international, "if one only knows one's own country's langauge, one's sense of things is nationalistic." the symbol of itself, its religion quest. williams, the thing in itself, the exact fact, the meter of the written word from the spoken word, its exact. 3) how to deal with pluralism; the harbor, los angeles's diversity of races, its intellectual development.

4) the magazines that i have liked in the small press world in this super, middle-class city which unlike any other city in america has a relationship not with necessarily but real america but to the planet. l.a. has a relationship with the planet. they are *momentum*, beginning with vol 1 no 1 march, 1974; *bachy*, the sensuousness of *chrysalis* in its beginning, *sunset palms hotel*, *little caesar*, i speak of these in seriousness, *temblor* & *caterpillar*, *sulfur*, i am beginning to name a few magazines that i liked & i hated, but they are on very high literary levels & the editors are knowledgeable in literature. also anarchism on a literary level. anything is permissable in a frame. i do not believe in physical violence. i make my living as an actor. some things i am old fashioned in, some things i learn new. we have new rhymers, new combinations of learning how to make a poem. a poet is a writer who has a corpus of work. poetry is redundant to the end of the last sentence because a poet makes works within poetry. the use of the word text is nothing new; poetry, the making of the writing about is centered in the text, the way the words are put together, is the form new, is there morality may be an outworn word harmony. the essence has been the

voice, the suffering harmony to express the inner text looking at a thing.
5) emphasizing the performer is anti-literary. 6) we learn concision
lucidity from h.d., the aphrodite of the long poem in the twentieth
century, the image off a northeast coast line childhood memory made
mythic in the shield of the charioteer at delphi, she was not the myth the
men made up. 7) take wilshire & drive west till you hit the ocean, tears
shed for her erring son, the sun above the bay its curving upward beach
road, super highway among the she said. 8) one editor has a.i.d.s one
gives grants, one forms a poetry cooperative one reads his poems in
nightclubs. 9) "take poetry out of the store fronts & put it in the
nightclub," tom waits told me fifteen years ago at beyond baroque west
washington venice. 10) its religion is still word. light begat. not the
cafes. not the sunsets. not the cars. the elemental word is the elements
itself.

    harry northup writing thoughts about the tradition of poetry in los
angeles what is its american connection what is new in poetry from l.a.
within a room of books & a tv in east hollywood.

l.a.f.d. ambulance

there were two cop cars, de longpre
& normandie, two cops standing outside

a blonde woman, clean, poor-looking,
leather coat, stylish, old, "could you
let me have some change to help pay
for my rent?"   sunset, next to ron's

two young black men dressed in blue
running suits, on the telephone, one,
one on the sidewalk walking toward
someone in a car i thought were
pimps
a heavy-set hooker on sunset bench
red shoes, black skirt, red shirt,
black coat, red-haired

two blocks down, a young woman star-
let like hooker across the pedestrian
lane, in front of cars, black mini skirt,
hair brown, straight slicked back,
black coat thrown around her
shoulders, tanned face, sleek
pushing her body into the street

he identified with me, trying to
separate, he has been sober for
78 days; i have been straight
for most recent two months, this
is the second time i bought some

i fall i fail i worry will it affect
him, i must be moderate i
pay his insurance, allowance, etc...

he has been chanting at n.s.a &
it has helped him & he has been
chanting at home, on vacation,
chanting for guidance, answers,
he has gotten positive support

when i come home after buying
gloves for my character, a
carpenter, with pigeons, a 3-story
house in a riverfront area, working
class, a dead daughter

i bought flowers, pink carnations
is it better to love one another
what a pretty color she said
& two bluebirds on snow, delicate
away from the religious into nature

12   11   89

the way of life & the radio

on the way home i listen to kpfk & a woman says "man despoils
nature & woman is nature & man destroys / holds down / cuts
down the grove in the old testament & says man hates woman &"
i think to myself that i have seen women treat nature in a
bad way & i think of the lovely images of mother & child /

mary & jesus, & i come home tell holly what i heard & she
says "o, that's an old cliche; nobody believes that anymore"
the bible taught me "respect your mother & father" "thou shalt
not kill" "thou shalt not steal" & i have sinned; but i hold
these & other moral laws in my mind / heart, nature is a child
& we are its death

12   18   89

hollywood actor

i get the job & make plans with inner emotions, his cap
he dresses in layers: thermal long underwear, flannel
shirt, heavy flannel shirt over that, brown quilted vest
his arms are free to swing the hammer & if/as the weather
gets warmer, he sheds

then i drive around, i pick up my son, take him to market
eat with him, give him his allowance; he's working now, so he
will have money

then its agony over the amount of time i spend watching tv
there are revolutions going on in middle eastern europe
tv is showing the world to the world, & changing it

& then i get ideas, people help me; i feed the cat & let
the pigeon in for an hour a day, he flies now, today i
wrongly thought i bent his wing, it was okay
he's a lebanon, mailman, messenger from lebanon
the armenian calls him, those are his pigeons, he got
divorced, had no place to keep them, he comes over once
a day

clean, sport coat, shirt, nice, slacks, sandals, well-fed

its the city that drives me crazy; i worry about giving
a pierre cardin three-piece suit to a salvation army thrift
shop & got the receipt for it & other things, later, when i
reached for a joint, i remembered i had stuck the eighth &
rolling papers in the inside pocket of the suit & i am
worried about being arrested for the grass in the coat pocket
in the suit i gave away

its the end of the year & i have an acting job in a movie
in february in pittsburgh & i have been working on the character
i am playing, through the pain & the suffering & its love.

12   19   89

back from a walk

we ate rice & chicken & cheese pie
went to the nuart with friends saw
"mystery train" came home two calls
on the answering machine one i had
envisioned earlier

the other night saturday i got a call
on the machine from my son he said
i am just calling to say hello & to
tell you that the manager is going
to make me a waiter like i was

hired for & i don't have to wash dishes
anymore

i was glad that my son had called me
like he said he would & also that the
news was good

i came into holly's room & said would
you read me about 30 pages from
your journal about when you get

back from a walk?   later i said i
will share my notebook with you & you
can read from your journal.   i'm
trying to teach you to be more open
& honest.

later she said my journal is private
& i am going to have women friends

12   26   89

"it's a shame there are no national poets" a writer said on tv

it's timing & a need for a national
poet
a man, a woman, a jew, an african-
american
a junkie, a christian, a professor,
academic or working man
communicative or obscure
ginsberg, wilbur, snyder,

i am talking about the strength in duty
love loyalty work equal opportunity

the work has been getting sparer
man at middle age desires fleshly
things sex food sensory things

when he tries to stand in loyalty
the plurality of our land
the heart is still in its honesty hand
work thrift loyalty love liberty

the individual remains important
coming into a need for unity community

i heard the poet of his american heart!

12   26   89

the eastern line

the #4 bus ran a red light
it was raining
my artist friend tells me about
bacon, "horrific, i'd say," he said
"twists the body" "photographs of
friends" to maim in private
my friend was taken to the galleria
where he was bought a cardigan
sweater, he bought himself two books
about picasso & francis bacon.

"you've seen california
now go back home" bumper sticker
a study of urban poets
the last hundred years
my son works at pizza hut
washington & lincoln, good tips
they hired him as a waiter
they had him work as a dishwasher
they made him a waiter.   he's happy
bought a pair of black leather shoes
at payless, pico & lincoln, for work.

i sit on bus benches
sunset, normandie to western,
i see the waiting postures of hookers
"they remove nokada blue"
or the dancing, almost naked
dark & white women; the dark
men around the bar, at tables.

                    12   29   89

stanley ave

the poetics for me was learning
to read young in the warmth of
the woman teaching me to read,
reading to me. stories of the father
& mother & brothers & sister, aunts,
grandparents, uncle, cousin, horses
& wagons, animals, farms, cities,
travel, school, work.

how will he eat without the rocks to
grind. i wrongly thought i had
broken the wing.

the roundness of the harmony & the
grasshopper shuts him off

it's my house, i thought of my
character & i've fucked up so much
& broke crying in my bedroom

"hope the panic subsides"
a painting on a mirror
a new tv on the installment plan
people carry their books under their
arms & talk to strangers
i take buses i walk i drive
but it is the city & we seek out
when we need our wants: the light
& pool & cat in the window den waiting
i got the code word in case i forget
to turn off the alarm before opening

12   29   89

running the clock down

it's a time to be an arrival
& a poet.
the fruit freezes & is lost unless it
is kept frozen till sold
i saw a bright star above a crescent
moon
the big tree on normandie was cut
into big sections & carried away in
a truck
its base & roots remain & the men
dig holes in various spots of the yard
armenian men stand & watch

the children, gloriously taking care
of younger ones yelling their name
over & over again, cadillacs, the
outdoor living, long florescent bulb
the snapping down of cards at bedtime,
midnight,
& the warriors are buried under the
interchanges.

i arrive home from being out & i
am blessed.   i sin & i ask for
forgiveness & the revolutions are the
cars, shakespeare bridge.

i have walked down a hollywood street
with health & love & observation.
a handful of corn dreams.
i sit at western & sunset, like i did in
new york, staring at old men talking.

12   29   89

the job of the poet

the first jobs i had: paper boy, 12,
clothing saleman, 15, 16 at two
men's stores, earlier field worker.

i see that olson's poetry, his vision,
its reality appears, is on the page.   the
experience felt & seen, inhabited.   the
way his poem "winter" turns its wintry
field into a metaphor for death, association
& an assessment of the modern age season.
speaking news is thrilling, his work is
clean & fresh, a truthfulness.   but it is
always music.   the way he constructs
words.   like whitman he is also general.

my son has a job now at pizza hut.
he bought a pair of black leather shoes
to wear at work.   "the boss likes me."
he is happy.   he is also sober for
ninety plus days.   i was for many
days, but i have scored three times
in the past month or so, a week.   i
have a deep sense of guilt in that,
worried about having a quarter of
grass, good, getting caught by the police
& thrown in jail.   i worry about not
being a good example to my son.

i am happy he works, i sit & read olson.

12   29   89

borders

people cross borders
ideas go across borders
food goes across borders
missiles cross borders
bullets cross borders
money goes across borders

love crosses borders
drugs go across borders
freedom crosses borders
cars & planes cross borders
ambassadors & soldiers
culture & checks
tv & radio cross borders
water is often used
as a border
corn & bird cross borders

1   10   90

holiday

the pigeon's out
lebanon, red
mailman, messenger
from lebanon

he steps out of
the cat cage
walks around
the bedroom

flies up to the
curtain rod, walks
along it, flies

to another golden
painted rod

he's so beautiful
to look at, up high

1   14   90

18

childbreaking
i told her 18
moon november
tarot card

hugging my heels
veil ship
take away

she ordered
vision after
relative rampage
she said great
& wrote it down

pieces meeting
solitude warmth
orange cat
red pigeon

how do we
hunger ourselves
together

two buses
to be understood
both going

his wings
will not be
disappointed

1   17   90

numbers

the 4th psychologist
my son has seen
maple center beverly hills
finished
8 sessions
ended philosophically
discussing siddhartha
my son mentioned struggle
finding his way
he was happy
sitting in a room
having worked that day
found a job at pizza hut
pays rent to his mom
30 dollars a week

he turns 21 tomorrow
he works makes good tips
plus $4.25 an hour
buys cassettes with his tips
rides the blue bus
right outside his home
6th & pico, gets on

pizza hut warm place
washington & lincoln
began job the week
after thanksgiving
he's happy he's working
he's friendly to people
gray pants, black leather shoes
pink striped short sleeved shirt
red cap with pizza hut on it

1   28   90

something that loves a wound

i believe that life
is the life.   a real
fear.   sympathy with wind.
the 17th c. poets have been
wounded by tv.
to be found indeed lord
an old friend called & asked
the helicopter above
a car door slamming
to believe life is cheap
requires fatality
an experience an ash tray
a bracelet
the weather has been cold
& the neighbors have
stayed inside
i read the 17th c. poets
to find grace, i find density.
an intricate, graceful wit
shunned, because he tries
himself: i believe in writing
a true sentence.   true
in its bewilderment: did you
hear a gunshot?   yes.   the
lights turned out, i looked
out into the street
nothing, & later more gunshot
sounds.
to find an angel in life
is to find a wall.

1   28   90

the door

to be able to write a good
clean, true sentence
like hemingway
& sustain the style, like he did,
for many books
sometimes i think everything
hemingway wrote was a metaphor
for writing
how close can you get
to the truth, to death
like *death in the afternoon*

he would like you saying that
a university english professor said

it's either hemingway
or stein, the two branches

no, they're both prose, he said
the poets have kept stein alive, i said

i taught my son to read with
simple declarative sentences
we read hemingway's short stories out
loud
nelson algren said hemingway all
the way, said he never went for
the bucks

1990, l.a., bedroom, east hollywood, color
tv, about to go work on a movie in
pittsburgh — the books i began with.

1   29   90

finally

in a town outside pittsburgh
sitting in a large room, honey
wagon — mark brought me my
clothes — same idea as mine
only gray & blue, old, faded

last night in the westin william
penn, 11th floor room, i could hardly
sleep—anxiety—felt high in the air
also an airplane flight feeling—
didn't know if i could come down

today in the van, tak, the cinematographer
asked me questions about
working in marty's first film
"who's that knocking at my door?"
the size of the crew, the cost. . .
made me feel good — he loved the film

i'm dressed, the heat is on, i'd
better concentrate on my part

2   8   90

first day shooting

jonathan said
harry, you look good

tak said
i like "who's that knocking. . ."
it's like what they taught
us in film school

mark said
oho, i'd better sew
that hole in your crotch

karen said
i recognize you
from your photos

there were others
some good, some bad

i'm in my costume
i am sitting in my room
i've visited my home
in the movie

it's gray out, cold
the heat is on
i wait for my scenes

2   8   90

plane home

when i finished shooting
jonathan wanted me to come
& say bye to him after
i changed clothes

he was warm & happy
about my work
he held me
said say hello to dylan
said jodie harry's leaving

i shook hands with tak
& jodie, she said
let's make it a fourth film soon

that night i was
coming out of the gift shop
& i saw the producer
i thanked him
he had just seen my dailies
& praised my work
the tall woman with him
said you were brilliant

i had trouble sleeping
as usual
ended up falling out
about 4 a.m.

i got up at 7:46
the alarm didn't go off
the wake-up service did not call

i had to rush around
to get orange juice & coffee
& pay my bills & check out
& catch a cab to the airport

it was the first time
i felt pressed for time
& began sweating

the job is completed
i worked with a great director
actress & cinematographer

this was the longest advance
i had ever gotten an acting job
three & a half months

it paid off
i had knowledge to work
with the pigeons
i contributed things
not in the script
created words & actions

i had learned to smoke
for "mr. bimmel"
& had practiced carpenter work
discarded both

this was my 29th film
i had not worked as an actor
for a year & three months

the one thing that happened
to me was that the night

before i was to do my scenes
i could not sleep
i had an anxiety attack

i was staying on the 11th floor
at the westin william penn
& i felt so high
like in an airplane
& it was like i would
never come down
a crazy eerie feeling

i think it had something to do
with the fact that i had not
worked as an actor last year
& that i needed to work & complete
an acting job before june 15th, 1990
in order to collect unemployment
which would be 190 dollars a week

so i was living behind
& thinking ahead
thank god i did good
my preparation was thorough
i worked with good people
who were gracious & friendly to me

it was a wonderful job
& once again i am thankful
to work as an actor

2   10   90

arrival

the first thing
i am going to do
when i get home
is to ask holly
to marry me

2   10   90

time

the one thing i have to learn
is how to accept the present
how to live in the present

working as an actor
one is tempted to look ahead
if i do good in this
this will happen
i could make this much money
if the movie or commercial
does well

it has to do with my not sleeping
thinking ahead
wanting to sleep fast
wanting the morning to come

five minutes ago
i looked at my watch: 12:30 p.m.
2½ more hours to go
till i arrive at lax

it caused me anxiety
not having control over time
being up in the air
wanting to be home
to be home safe

my writing helps me
to understand the present time
to release time into an eternal
present

2   10   90

a shaman purpose a minute

have you ever seen
so many shamans in your life?
a shaman to heal
to promote
to do personal relations.

how long before men & women
treat each other with courtesy?
the same for blacks & whites.
bell boy, bell boy
we can be beowulf together
after the ceremony.

you lily white ass the black man says
the whites were destructive
the romans, egyptians
we live in a conservative time.

i do personal relations
therefore i am a poet
i am a lawyer, a therapist
therefore i am a poet

the young men at the fountain
they want us to believe
the world is rich with poets
& the secretary poet says
the people at the office
treat me nicer now that they know
i am a famous poet.

& the middle-class poet eats at city
restaurant, wears styled clothes
says poetry is beautiful lies

& its helicopters against helicopters
& one man is poet of shit & one of
sex & slave, university one

pound said poetry should be as well
written as prose
his penelope was flaubert
said hugh selwyn mauberley
i say poetry should be as well
written as film
the many hours, the vision
hollywood a high-technical proficiency

the poet attacks with slang,
with epic, songs sacred, lyrical
i am so shy about this
its the wedding vow interlaced
with an external plural plural

we are beset with youthful gods
of yellow hair & tight pants, black,
boots with silver, shirt open

it is a castle that is hungry
& declarative sentences are not
enough & exotic languages are
not enough & popularity & tv
is people magazine
we watch people on tv

the black cab driver/owner
from kenya knew about provence
known for its poets
you're a good driver opened
the conversation on western

please me then with the death of god

covered by blue waters
a man old appears in blue robe
on a throne chair in a chariot
above in the sky clouds part
the ghost is the female

2   22   90

waves sameness hope

throat, woman, end of her nose
orange red hair, street teeth glasses
enormous momentary sleeves begging
beyond the profound restless
nice dead rather home
recognized mathematical residual
moons stars thighs
dog resting bright roots
recently wrecked traffic eyes planted
gate strength winterlong satyrs
fertile reconciliation senses your face

april 11, 1990

the days of my life

the days of my life
are a pink rose

there is a lady
in a green gown
& a heart around her

i love you like i
love the hands above

it's a springy rabbit
on a roller skate
the rabbit stands
on its front feet

it's a red haired woman
standing on two horses
coming into town
a glow

it's commonplace
& it's a boy sitting
on earth a blue
circle on his face

april 11, 1990

clearing everything out

the irrational telling the
irrational thing that is going
to happen

scholars, windows flung open
puma princes
the three goddesses

law unto the dark
she leaned back against the machine
watching the morning game show

cleaning & money, sexual
the movie-goer sat in his car
on vermont
watching a pair of young lovers
both women hugging their men
around their necks, kissing them

two armenian men lounge outside
a liquor store, one works in

they are cunning, work, patience

april 18, 1990

poem preference

i admire the in-the-earth, gem-like poem
i stand before you in my ground, soil, a
city; a city whose diction: freeways
telephones fine restaurants youthful
interchanges; i stand before you in my
lean middle-aged spirit.   it has to be
real because that is the movies.

sunset strip, melrose, la brea, the lane
changes

barry & i went downtown to gorky's for coffee & conversation

last night i saw a flame of fire
come out of a deep green dragon
mouth surrounded by a black indenta-
tion
it was the darkness telling me
i had gone far enough in drugs

something which is haunting

"hang on to your hats, the
armenians are loose!"

"boy, they are really whooping
it up, aren't they?"

i walked to the new thrifty's
at western & sunset & bought a black
dress belt & a pair of gray socks.

at one p.m. we are going downtown
to see the blessing of the animals.

tomorrow i will pick dylan up at five p.m.
& bring him here for an easter turkey
dinner.

the son will be the best man

the helicopters are always
above us; gang guys hang out
sit on the wall under trees
next to our apartment

moderation, compassion, honesty
as much as possible, danger vulnera-
bility

the young man took his sport coat,
dress pants, white shirt to the cleaners
his father took the boy's shoes
to be shined; the young man
talked happily about his father's
"big wedding" "i'm going to buy
you a present, & holly" the father
picked out a tie for his son
the son will be the best man

the man & the woman made love
lovingly, delicately, rushing
the man had bathed first

she was beautiful & clean
in two days, they are going to
see the dodgers play the pirates
a celebration of her 52nd birthday
in twelve days they are getting
married

april 30, 1990

may poem

my situation is this: i like unity.
being a movie actor, i have to deal
in reality. observing humans. basing
the imagination in the real physical.
transcending or not transcending reality.

could it be that all the talk about poetry
within the poem is that it is talk
among poets — because the audience is
very small. so the talk is affected by
the prose poem of the symbolists, its long-
line prose thrust by the language poets.
and the thought gets more eclectic. a
juxtaposition of literary impressions &
gossip. the many fragments of the 20th
century.

some are tired of the william carlos
williams real concise, physically real
perceptions, concrete some may say;

some say the writing is an escape from
the real;

some are tired of arguing over what
is real;

some imitate joyce, *finnegan's wake,*
ulysses; some stein; some hemingway

some are tired of the modern flatness;

could it be that this life is an illusion;

some say it is all madison avenue,
madison avenue could sell any book
of poetry if it chose to;

some say jerusalem; some say i am
not to be fettered in spirit or in
verse;

my aim is not to be horse whipped
desired,
it was rainy that day
to be constantly worried about the
external; the cars on mariposa —
stopping, driving past, give me fear,
paranoia comes from a fact.
but it is often then empty, ill-con-
centrated —- the mind is then on
another external, fact, unknown
spirit-time

may   3,   1990

late night

tomorrow we are going to order
a wedding cake for twenty-five

we are going to order flowers
"ten days left," a friend said
this afternoon at the market
he asked me if i was getting nervous
& i said no

in many ways, holly is taking a
chance on me because i am not
working; i can open an unemployment
claim a month after we marry
that scares me a little bit

there was a big commotion the other night
a helicopter going around & around
above us to the north slightly
the cops had cordoned off the block
three houses north & across the street
each way each corner each alley

a male hispanic stole a car
was chased by cops, dumped the car
ran, was pursued, dogs brought in
they caught him in forty-five minutes

to me it is a continual, an unfolding
she sleeps, the cat above her head
on the pillow

may 3, 1990

it is almost midnight

we went to panos pastries
hollywood & kenmore
looked at cakes, priced them
we went to sorbonne on hillhurst
did the same

we went to farmers market
ordered a lemon chiffon wedding cake
two tiers

we ordered 3 boutonnieres & 2 corsages

holly made andy's sauce, rigatoni &
a salad

i watched 2 basketball playoff
games; holly ironed
after supper, she talked to phoebe
on the phone for over an hour

i called dylan & said i'd meet him
at his place monday & have him
try on his new white shirt to
see if it fits, & take him his newly
shined black loafers, & see if the
tie matches his sport coat & slacks

holly sleeps, it is almost midnight
it's hot in hollywood; in a week
from tomorrow, holly & i marry

may 4, 1990

honeymoon in pismo beach

the ring on my finger
postcards from hearst's ranch,
the monterey aquarium, old
port inn —
the movement in my legs
from highway 101 & 1

a bay memory
salmon butterflied
walks along a clean beach
a sunset seen from the pier
in pismo beach

ducks within reaching distance
the softness of her body

driving the cliffs of big sur
downward on the outside
a test of nerves

pure ocean memory
paws at the whiskers
of the sea otters
brisk bay air
clean motel walls
the best bite of a clam
i ever tasted

i picked up a duck egg
from the parking lot of a 7 eleven
& took it to the bank of a nearby inlet
placed it on the grass

may 18, 1990

a vision

last night i had a vision
of a shark in a frame
with a rose growing out
of its body

5   24   90

memorial day week-end

we walked to a thai
restaurant, mini-mall
kingsley & sunset
lavender, gray, mint-green
holly had chow mein with shrimp
pad thai with shrimp for me

at 9, i turned on amc
& watched "love is a many splendored
thing"
holly joined me at 9:40

we enjoyed the movie
she asked me if i want to go
to church in the morning
i said wake me at 8, i'll see

memorial day week-end
i am almost finished with a bio
on william carlos williams
holly sleeps in bed
the cat sleeps on a green chair

the candle & the skyscraper
one lighted & one dark
red blushing flowers

may 26, 1990

sports bar

5 tv's in the sports harbor
all tuned to the portland/phoenix
playoff game
men & women watching
others playing pool, foosball, pop-shot,
shuffleboard
eating, drinking, talking
yelling when their team made a
good play

dylan & i watched the first half
i ate a cheeseburger & fries &
drank a budweiser
he drank coffee

i took him home at half-time
came back & watched the second half

it was the first time i had been in
a sports bar
it was fun

"you should be here at 10 a.m. on a
sunday — 5 tv's all turned to a
different game"

after the game, which the trail-
blazers won, i drove to the pier
& walked to its end — saw a mexican
fisherman let a crab freely walk
& then tumble over the side
back into the night water

may 30, 1990

celebration skins

i get so paranoid after smoking
a joint; i turn on "so what"
by miles davis — it soothes me step
by step

it's saturday in june
my love brings two photographs
one in a stunning green & brown
elegant thin stone frame
sets it on the speaker
we have been married three weeks
it's cooling out in the big city

it begins with a single real thing
movies are in my heart & movies
we actors talk about: year, director,
actors, story, scenes, shots, days worked,
dominating plays, the studying
in new york, method acting,
coming to hollywood, what year, joys
of study & work, stories.

then friends come, a poet, a high
school teacher, a psychologist, a
grade school special ed. teacher,
an opera lover; this is the city
& young couples, single women, armenians,
a french woman, two nebraska people.

it soothes me, like leaves & venetian
blinds shut almost.
the river, the railway & the car.

june 2, 1990

the body of my wife

the prettiest thing i ever saw
was my wife's body

i love to kiss her lips, hold her
body, touch her back, the lower back,
bone & curve.

i love to lick & suck her pussy.

i love to come in her
i love it when she gets on top
we fuck, she fucks me, i fuck her,
we fuck

i love her mind & her hair, her food
& clean, washed bed sheets, warm bed

at night in los angeles, "a simple
prayer" on the radio, my favorite song
of all time, a man says, "the ravens"

in a bedroom next to the street

they bow in their humility
this body, this brief existence.

i have described her body as french
vanilla ice cream & as a riverboat
wheel, or the curves of the desert
well, so do the secrets of the heart.

june 3, 1990

marriage poem 1

a thing does not have
to be viewed as an
acquistion. there is
a vulnerability living
in the city. go
fuller into the dark-
ness. a man sits in
his car, looks out at
trains, tracks, road,
river. another man
unlocks a gate &
drives his car through.
an attempt at healing
so, its an info heart
he fears the journey
wants to be nourisher,
protector but tries
to speak his truth. a
quiet inner feeling.
it means there is a
value cleanliness. it
hungers for the bath,
the bed, breath. the
story begins with a
man recently married,
twelve years love, he
opens a new claim of
unemployment, the
maximum payment, has
a part in a movie
coming out this fall,
poet actor husband
father friend. and
the female friend says

me woman 1990 white
i'm weird. the fields
from which it came, &
its skin pulled back
by sections, showing
its juicy green body
there is love & work in
the city & there are
paranoias, frailties.
humilities he said i
was thinking of it
as a title for a book
of poetry. friends
& family have been
warm & giving to us
after our wedding.
raising the emotional
& intensity level. he
seeks solace then in
studying w.c. williams,
pound, h.d., hart crane,
whitman, dickinson.
he watches "wages of
fear" on tnt & loves
it. clouzot. so it is
solace born out of
value of real physical
details. i love the
solidness of h.d.'s poetry
its sense of personal
& mythic. its clean-
liness. i had a good
family, loving. he prays
for those he loves, he
asks for help in under-
standing & learning to
love his opposites. to
develop cohesiveness,

he walks up & down
vermont, l.a.c.c. to
franklin & 7 eleven on
one corner, house of
pies on southwest. he
goes out into the world
& gets love, work, warmth,
gets criticized, hammered.
and back up and back
up. he hears talk
at the college grille
about the "real angelenos"
a man criticized a man.
others can't hold their
tongue, water & use
to conserve & yet to be
wild. the woman says
me female 1990. ask
me. i am your mother,
ask me. and he sees
in her himself. in
her seeking. friends,
they sit in newly-
married friend's home.
with graciousness &
talk of sacred texts,
talk of personal joy
& drama.

6   3   90

solace

when the city life gets to me,
i put on "patricia" by art
pepper & its tenderness soothes
me out

this is the time when the single, middle-
aged woman has repressed everything
to its boundaries
& all hell venom breaks forth

she stabs the old armenian gard-
ener with a fork in his chest

the armenian family drive her
nuts, she calls them gypsies
she argues against joyful things
she sees in the world: courteous
love, boundless human contact,
the mess of it all as shared she
lives quietly for months, is always
snarly, a few times sensible, she
explodes at the landlord, she listens
to opera, she falls asleep in front
of her tv, i call her to please
turn the tv down, its 1:30 a.m.

in our land, we yearn for courtesy,
friendliness, neighborliness
it came the morning after a night
of food, celebration, love, friendship,
drunkenness, talk of god, gods, society,
fear, creativity, a common seeking
ground.

june 3, 1990

poetry philosophy

something has its own life

its exciting to watch a cat watch
a nearby bird

when play acting becomes reality

must always come down to the sensual &
spiritual
it is real because the word & its use are
real

there are birds & sunlight, inner light
greenery & animals

a chair & a radio, record player. . .
time to seek solace through words

one man is a christian in a secular society
one woman expressed what she once thought
normal is now weird

something to bind schisms with gentleness

june 6, 1990

it's the first

it's the earth
must join
with thunder

voice dead within
must flourish
springtime

a bird distracting
you from its egg

a summer stock
company in woodstock
vermont, 17 of us
living in a converted
barn
my ex-wife tried
to kill herself
she felt so alone
repertory company
i did three leads
in a row, we fucked
once in a field
next to a field
of morgan horses
between two rocks
some light green grass
& stubble

it must join with
rubble, it must join
with blood, with human

june 7, 1990

rent & reading

i sat in the back of the tent
behind the revolving wall
& i blew up colored balloons &
tied them on the hooks
it was a narrow aisle i sat in
seventh grader — i read *the life
of lou gehrig* on that job

holly walked in & gave me
many loves and other plays by
william carlos williams "you can
have it now; you don't have to wait
till father's day if you don't want to"

i was in the navy for three years
& never went aboard ship
boot camp in san diego, 3 months in
imperial beach sweeping & swabbing
the long tunnel with 16" guns at
end rounded end, 6 months radio school
san diego, 3 days treasure island, 14 months
pearl harbor radio operator, 10 months
waihiawa

i sold clothes & i worked as a
messenger

she got me the book i wanted
i've been reading his early & later
poems & criticism — i've been
wanting to read a play of his
wcw died march 4th, 1963

june 7, 1990

ballgame friend

it was very nice going to the baseball
game with jack wassil last night
he came on time
he was dressed neat & clean
he was thankful & enthusiastic

we went in his air-conditioned 1982 buick
i had the tickets i had bought
he paid for parking
i gave succinct, clear directions

we talked about our wives & children
we talked with knowledge about baseball
we laughed, yelled, clapped, took our
caps off for the singing of the national
anthem
we both got a free dodger cap — it was
cap night
the weather was perfect
he bought me a beer
i bought him unsalted peanuts
we had good seats on the top deck above
home plate

we looked at the downtown skyline
we talked about pittsburgh where he's
from
we stood & sang "take me out to the
ball game" during the seventh inning
stretch
we watched fernando win
bringing his record to 5-5
we saw eddie murray homer
we drank hot choclate

we enjoyed the game & each other's
company

i asked him to come in for a minute
& i gave him "the little mermaid"
cassette for his six year old daughter

go to fountain, make a left
go to western, left & make a
right onto the 101 north
just south of the gas station

thanks for the coasters with the N

june 20, 1990

the ragged vertical
12-5-90
to
12-27-91

sign

sign unknown, darkened by
light, protected
the clock protects us
eight oriental women in a row
she was a tigress last night
in our love making
she has been kissing me lately,
spontaneously
she's going to go away for four
days soon — to the mountains
& to an island

he pulls the curtains &
she goes to bed, he shuts
the door — afternoon

she makes animal noises
& her body lifts
he tongues her cunt
he bubbles spit into her cunt

they speak with their bodies
like animals, with abstract
flowers of image pleasure
a house where harps were made
a white cat with a black tail

i look for signs at the market
among men speaking morse
code, spelling out waffles
among congratulations for a
one man show, among talk
of dying, among juice
extractors & plastic bottles

there was a house & in that
house, a poet wrote to another
poet expressing his sadness
over the other having a.i.d.s.
he cried, as he wrote, tears
shaped like lilies — white with
contrary violet

he looks for signs in trees &
birds, in poets' meetings
& poets' festivals, in poets'
arguments over politics
he wants his hand to be
kindness in its sleeplessness

when i first went to new york

to try to make it as an actor
the bus station was at either
34th st or 50th, off eighth
it seemed, that was 1963
march, i believe; i went across
the street to a white rock, or
white castle, & a good-looking man,
about thirty, hair combed back
he sat between two young lovely women
his name was stag roper & he told them
about working as an extra in a movie
in hawaii
it could have been one year earlier
when i came from nebraska to audition
for & get a job as an apprentice at
lake whalom playhouse, fitchburg, mass.
guy palmerton was the producer
he had once produced four summer
stock companies in the northeast
he lived in a hotel on 52nd & broadway
but the guy in the cafe was heroic to me
he was a live actor who had acted in a movie
& the women looked at him like a hero, too
later, i lived in the keystone hotel, 36th
& eighth, the park wald on 58th, off sixth
the keystone was brief, cockroaches, dirty
toilet, army blanket, narrow, dreary,
i lived at the cort for two years, & the
park wald for a year
while i studied acting; i studied acting
for five straight years, that's all i
thought about, acting, theatre, movies,
plays, books about theatre, history

walking through intersections repeating lines
memorizing lines
no one knows much about the ordinary working
movie actor, from the littlest extra to the
biggest movie star
to go to new york in '62 & get a summer stock
job & return to stock a second summer, to study
& to work in two films & to go to movies at
mid-morning in mid-manhattan
there were many apartments that i lived in
many jobs: waiter, counterman, messenger, clerk
typist, phone salesman
it's a dream to work in the movies &
my dream began in new york

12   6   90

sign —

sign — a long crucifix being
hoisted up, a man on it, tied.
white skeleton dancing in
the dark.
neon horns, in a circle, six,
creme light. twirling.
a man on a horse, riding
past a cactus, the sun setting.
a face with a mask, cowboy
hat. the pointed finger,
eyes holes of light.
a round face & the inner
circles closing. a still
man with a white mustache,
cowboy hat. many stars en-
circling him. going back
home, a thin cowpoke. stars
above. dark blue sky.

a

it was a line then the candle had
fallen

the lights in front of the garage had
went past warmth

he saw a scent of his past in a matching
blue royal coal

it was then that his friend had gone
a blue-yellow flower, opening in front
of the large sun, a bonnet

in romanticism remained ruins
love & justice wed, my memory of her

pronouns big as the stars in night
if it is identical then it fails

the actor memories — to sell for a
picture, it is a deepest dream in
me to work as an actor, & my
memory of it is eight months

there is the memory then, of ruins,
of glimpsed mortality, she said,
"i came to los angeles to live,"
never a fan of nathanael west,
whom strasberg said had written
the best book on hollywood, *the day
of the locust.*

and each summing up is a failure.
because the line was on wood & white
fallen flatness in a circle, one
standing, one fallen, music, shadow.

the chant

i began chanting *the bhagavad
gita*, translated by ann stanford,
out loud today, in my car, at
home. the dualities stagger me.
friendship, paranoia. clarity,
bewilderment. disintegration &
the coming together. the
wedding & the old canadian
finding his cows.
rhythm harmony melody
she sucked me off & it
felt wonderful
she was crouched, her body
close to the bed
she sucked me off for a
long time
it came from the spiritual
she got on top of me
& we fucked
it made me feel great, happy
one hand goes away
& later comes back to the
other's hand — the white
& the black — the man &
the woman — it goes back
a long way — they fuck —
they sleep — he reads writes
into the night — she rises
early — walks — eats —writes
they play together
they listen to one another

the brokenness

i would fall asleep among the green shaded lamps
on the long, smoothly worn library tables
while reading brecht, clurman, stanislavski, williams,
miller, shakespeare, ionesco... "the drums of night,"
&chekhov, "the three sisters"
it all goes back to college in nebraska
where i fell passionately in love with the theatre
began to read as many plays as possible
as much about the history of the theatre as i could
i saw plays by saroyan, webster, congreve, even plays
by the greek dramatists

in the twenty-two years that i have lived in los angeles
i have seen two plays that i have thought were good:
"the shaper," by john steppling & "the common pursuit,"
by simon gray

my first play in community theatre was in "time out for
ginger" at age sixteen, i was "george" in "our town,"
another community theatre production direction of connie
madsen, a short, powerfully-voiced, knowledgeable, chain-
smoking, passionately-lover of theatre, woman
make your voice reach to the back row, she said

in high school, i was the male lead in the jr. class play,
"headin' for a weddin'"
i won the "i speak for democracy" speech contest three
years in a row, each contestant had to write a ten-minute
speech & deliver it, my style was oratorical

i have done one play in l.a., "fool for love," i played
the father, ghost, i got good reviews in *the l.a. times*
& *dramalogue*, rehearsed for a month, played for a month

weekends, i would sit in my hotel room & read play after
play
i would go to every broadway, off-broadway play i could
many free tickets from equity
since living in los angeles most of my activity centers
around movies, tv & poetry
acting & poetry are my main two work areas
they consume me

the brokenness is not working in a film since february
the brokenness is not working as an actor all last year
the brokenness is that i made sixteen thousand last year
& it gave me the illusion that i was working in the industry

i read play after play in the fifth avenue library i got
tired fell out briefly came to began reading where i left off

12 27 90

the sidewalk

i would walk from the upper west side
to chinatown
or all over the west forties
theatres automats
eating snails in black bean sauce
69 bayard street

the sidewalk is then the heaven
i walked crosstown & i walked downtown
my friend max the artist
we met in summer stock in massachusetts
he drew me a map
fifth avenue down the middle
sixth & up to the left the west
madison park & on to the right east
numbers down — downtown
up — uptown

the sidewalk i walked on
in my suit with my briefcase
photos resume trade papers notebook brush
end up at the automat
or a movie 10 a m on 42nd st
running into people on the street i knew
actors i met in summer stock
from acting class on 54th st

stopping at equity seeking casting news
getting free theatre tickets to brecht
american musicals genet
i saw kazan on 47th west of broadway
tennessee williams in jim downey's on 8th
i took the staten island ferry to get away

subways bookstores cafes movies parks libraries
hospitals clothing stores bands bridges rivers

i journey the sidewalk past windows under lamps
in rain walking from 25th & tenth to washington
square park at 4 a m writing as i was walking

12   31   90

when will you be somewhere

one day until january 15, 1991
the deadline for iraq to withdraw

the written word, a silver cup,
music cassettes, rolls of pennies

to help him get back on his feet
maybe a month before he surfs again

the democratic side is open & divided
unified "of the united states"

joyce, movie reviews, the news about
the persian gulf crisis on cnn

communications faster than protocol
one man asked for a national day

of prayer, pray for god to guide us
give us strength: each side evokes god

iraq says we will not surrender
as if she were an outlaw, had done wrong

was on the run by digging in
will you attack israel yes, absolutely yes

aziz replied if iraq is attacked by the u.s.
the u.s. is the judge & executioner

the tv countdown, the tv war
not to the real men & women desert shield

military power, oil power, religious power
the shield of diversity, hunger & greed

does a circle permit rape, plunder, killing

1   14   91

its still a time

i feel better now than when i walked in
there has been, is, will be people who like to hang
around like people, according to race, age, religion

social, sexual, political ones think little of the old
the old tradition of poetry: freedom against tyranny
freedom against aggression: it has its own freedom
the muse :surrender. take its own root in its calling

sappho, homer, hesiod, through chaucer, blake, emily d.
whitman taught us that the body of woman, of man sacred
people are fighting now for social power, using sex
as sacred stone
i offer the stone to be what was good in the past & carried
into the here & now
flaubert, cezanne, stein
if we fight, let us fight for the right to witness selfexiles
within urban poverty of spirit & guilt
i am no more than the lowest man in our city, cabbie, cop,
homeless, criminal; i am no better than a woman, nor she me
except in our gift, our work, the time spent in language

language is a song & it is breath
angry, rageful, desperate, silenced, curvy & hard
the muse is not the muse of power, the fountain venus however
but poetry is more than eight, elderly immigrants sitting on
the bus bench on western & sunset speaking a foreign tongue
it is humanity it is brotherhood it is community

i am also a prince & a brother   :for the movies hail light
to play a bad guy, a good cop,   its to participate in drama
to enter into a song one does not need a cause
nature the bee the honey the flower is not an empty glass

nor is it dirty nor guilty nor alone but dies

except for the use of my kindness i am an unknown
a man sitting on the back of a bus being a witness to humanity
told i cannot write what i witness because i witnessed hatred
a stranger on a big city bus treating others in a mean way with
words & when i presented the sight with its words
the immigrants are always the ones with songs in their hearts
the drunken indian & the nebraska boy played baseball junior
league went into the navy boyhood friend he reached out &
grabbed the fast pitched ball with his bare right hand
speaking is not fighting but i can fight with words
i have been writing poetry for twenty-five years & i will
continue to write what is in my heart & my vision

3   18   91

april poem

third day in, residuals my one incoming payment
money for may bills, a couple of hundred more

as i wrote down two words on the front page of *reporter*
"what did you just write?" an actor asks in the market
while another actor flipped through the magazine twice
discussing the gross & number of theatres a hit i'm in

one man at another time says "fuck that movie" when a
trailer i'm in for a movie comes on the tv
but most of the reviews have been great

many people have said good things to me about my acting
in "the silence of the lambs"
holly & i went to the premiere in century city
red carpet dozens of photographers
it looked like marilyn monroe landing at idlewild
all the photographers' lights going off strobe lights
when jodie foster & anthony hopkins arrived

the director jonathan demme drew his arms around me
gave me a warm hug said "you are wonderful in the movie"
i introduced him to holly
bruce davison came up to me afterwards in the lobby
said "you were very moving," another actor came up &
spoke quietly "there was a longing in your face, you
must have only had seven or eight lines, but the scene
seemed very long & full" "you were up there on the screen
like a house" another call

two auditions in the last two months, one after the movie
release on february fourteenth valentine's day

quietly i go on about my work: seeking acting work, acting
poetry, writing & reading
learning about narrative, how is it spiral or how is it
straight, accounting, recounting
my journey is that: i am an actor
my journey so far has begun in 1962 when i went to new york
city to audition for summer stock
begun as a professional
because before there was community theatre, high school plays,
college, a passion born for theatre, reading plays & theatre
history

because lately there has been a burrowing, warmth, bed, movies,
love, family, animal, nature, seaside, library

                              4   3   91

absolute

i went over & kissed the cat
on the lips, she tried to bite
me on the lips
my wife is in morro bay

night i hear the clock
i miss her face & her hair
her belly, legs, breasts, neck, hands
lips & tongue & our cheeks against

the beautiful men & women on the bus
sleeping, smiling, sharing, kindness
red shoes & gold chain around an ankle
short gold skirt, hispanics, african
americans, young anglo with a skate-
board — his baseball cap on backwards

moving through the city on a bus

june 5, 1991

hollywood learning

i read *a life* by kazan
talk about his theatre & film work
to fellow actors
when asked which country did he hold first
camus said "i love my country but i love
my mother more" (france & algeria)
lee hickman is dead
his poetry is alive
kazan kazan kazan kazan kazan
he fucked a lot of women
hes a hell of a writer
he named names to continue working
schulberg did the same
"on the waterfront" his best its about
flawed hero
the television we all talk political correctness
the 90s is a composite of the 60s & the 70s
civil rights movement free speech movement
women's movement anti-vietnam movement
the woman who got prayer out of the schools
many things that started in the 60s
were never fulfilled in the 70s — a vacuum
kazan was the top director in the 40s & 50s
he saw a lot of death
one poem of ferlinghetti's ends with death
twenty-nine times
the beat poets came along at a good time
post world war two
a sense of buoyancy
america at its highest
"i'll kick yah eye"
to say what you mean
in its simplest way

its easy to speak educated
to live life in its fullest
while dying instead of dwelling on the dying
the fervor then is this mind its broken
sentences from the time between commercials
the overlays of sporting events
the supreme court taking away pieces of privacy
in louisiana in indiana on buses in florida
the 50s was a time of repression &
there were some great movies made "shane"
"from here to eternity" "on the waterfront"
& last night i got the news my oldest brother
has cancer of the stomach — lymphoma —
he went to college on the g.i. bill
was on an oil tanker in pearl harbor
when it was bombed
these are thoughts i have these days
my brother has the greatest blood with me

june 22, 1991

you ask how i can write what i do

lee came to my reading at the iguana
right around the corner from where he lived
"solid," he said

holly & i went to visit him at the presbyterian
hospital on vermont; it was raining
lee thin, with gray beard, beautifully his
aesthetically, austere distillation.

charles was there, taking care of him
lee was unhappy about the service
"if charles was my nurse here; i'd rather stay
here"
his window faced south, 12th floor

we invited charles & lee to dinner
because of lee's illness, they could not come

once, during reverie, lee said, "aren't we
supposed to have dinner with holly & harry"
weeks after it had passed

"he was handsome & youthful-looking, the way
we knew him in new york, right before he died"

i knew him downtown manhattan, midtown, knew
him on woody trail, hollywood blvd at gardner,
silver lake, letters from san francisco, north
hollywood

"you were in town & you didn't come to my poetry
reading!" he said

we sat at my white kitchen table in santa monica
& west hollywood discussing open form, closed
form, the long poem; he listened, he thought,
many times he bent forward as if in prayer, his
hands together near his chin, mouth, a cigarette
in his right finger & thumb, he was handsome,
erudite about poetry, great observer, great mind

it was almost surreal he died at 6:30 a.m., sunday,
may 12th, 1991, the light went out, two lights
remain, these words are in shadow, a melody lifts
i touch the base of his memory & it is a chin &
hair, long, combed, glasses, fair skin, bright
eyes

7   10   91

*WORKING
WITH
SCORSESE*

"Who's That Knocking At My Door?" (1967)

Last February when I was working on "The Silence Of The Lambs" in Pittsburgh, Tak Fujimoto, Demme's long-time ace cinematographer, told me how much he loved Scorsese's first film "Who's That Knocking At My Door?" He began asking me questions about the movie & said, "That's the way they taught us to make a film in film school."

I said, "It was a small crew. A cameraman, Michael Wadleigh — who directed 'Woodstock' — shot it. There was a lighting man & a sound man & maybe one or two others. I remember Scorsese standing behind the camera — like D. W. Griffith. We shot my scene — I played the rapist — who raped the female lead, Zena Bethune. It was at night & in the snow. Winter, 1967. We shot it in New Jersey at Haig Manoogian's farmhouse. He was the head of the N.Y.U Film School & a producer of the film. He was Marty's teacher. 'Raging Bull' is dedicated to him. We waited in the house until it got dark. The others ate pasta. I sat in another room thinking about the rape scene. Being a theatre actor, I thought of it as a long, enraged arc of a scene. But the lesson came to me that film is shot in pieces. The drive up the country road with Zena Bethune next to me. Cut. Back up. Over again. Then the turn into the farmhouse road. Turn the lights out. Turn the car off. Turn to her & begin kissing her. Lock the passenger's side door. Then the rough stuff. Forcing myself on her. A tumble out into the snow & field after she got the door open. Hitting her. Dragging her up the embankment into the car. Tearing her nylons off. Her dress up. On & on the rape. All done in pieces. I remember once hitting her head on the inner top of the door frame as I was thrusting her back into the front seat. Scorsese has always loved violence & this was a violent scene. But he has also always loved his actors & he was compassionate & caring in the way he looked after Zena & me.

"The film originally cost $35,000 & then with some added sexual scenes in the center & p.r. in the next year or two took the cost to

$75,000. It got a great review by Roger Ebert of a Chicago paper & a superb review in *Time*.

"Thelma Schoonmaker was his editor. People around him then thought of him as a born film-maker."

I saw it out here at the Vagabond in '68, or '69 released as "J.R." Looking at that movie, you can see that his ambience is authentic.

"Boxcar Bertha"

"Boxcar Bertha," Scorsese's second feature, is a Roger Corman film. I played "Deputy Sheriff Harvey Hall." My character calls Bernie Casey racist names & beats up David Carradine with a blackjack in jail. Later, Barbara Hershey lures me into the woods after I had fixed a flat tire for her & Carradine hits me over the head with a shovel & Carradine & Casey escape.

One time during rehearsal — the week before shooting began — Carradine began yelling about something — this was not during a scene — & Scorsese took him aside & said, "Please don't yell because it makes me sick & then if I get sick, I can't work." This story was told to me by Vic Argo who was there (he has been in five of Scorsese's films).

Personally, I have never heard a raised voice on a Scorsese set. Scorsese always talks to his actors with love & gentleness.

"Mean Streets" (1973)

Scorsese gave me the part of "Jerry" in "Mean Streets." In the script, "Jerry" was given a party before he went away to the service. He was wearing a suit in the scene. He was given a good time & then he fell over drunk, face-first into his cake.

I told Marty that I would like to have "Jerry," dressed in a uniform, be home from the service. That way I could stand out from the others. I had heard Marty being interviewed & he had said "Violence always erupts in the background." This was in line with my conception of my character. I had told Marty that while all these guys were philosophizing — "Art thou King of the Jews?" & "I come to bring order" — I'll turn their picnic into a nightmare. I said that I will destroy the cake that they have given me, rip up the tables & attack a chick. Marty loved it. Pauline Kael said that Marty likes to put actors in a scene & let things erupt of their own volition. I asked the prop man how many cakes he had & he said two. I told Kent Wakeford, the cinematographer, that there were only two cakes for the two takes, so please keep me in frame. Everything worked great. Marty loved my idea & the execution went great. He cut from this violent scene to "Charlie" dancing in the next room with the girl I'd attacked. Violence juxtaposed with tenderness. Vincent Canby in *The New York Times* said the scene where "Jerry" (the Vietnam vet) tears up his own homecoming "is one of the most mysteriously sorrowful moments in recent American cinema."

Before the scene began, Marty came up to me & Harvey & I said to him, "Marty, I don't have any lines," & he said, "Don't worry about it, film is visual."

The writer Mardik Martin who wrote it with Marty came up to me at a party after the movie had opened & said, "You brought things to that part that weren't in the script." He thanked me.

"Mean Streets" is still my favorite movie by Scorsese. I love the energy & the penetrating camera & the great "Charlie"/ "Johnny Boy" relationship. Scorsese, as has been pointed out — somewhat like Godard in "Breathless" — is the center two characters in an inner way, but he is also in the film as a character & then the first person becomes the third person & he shoots "Johnny Boy" at the end. Pauline Kael has called the film "a true original, & a triumph of personal filmmaking." She adds, "The director, Martin Scorsese, shows us a thicker-textured rot than we have ever had in an American movie, & a riper sense of evil."

"Alice Doesn't Live Here Anymore" (1974)

After I had settled in my motel room in Phoenix, the night before I was to work in "Alice Doesn't Live Here Anymore," I went to eat & on the way back from dinner, I ran into Marty Scorsese & Sandra Weintraub, his love & Associate Producer. She said, "Here's Marty's good luck piece." He asked me to come into his motel suite. In the front room, there was one book opened: It was *The Complete Poems & Prose of William Blake.* Marty opened the script, looked at my scene & said, "We'll just keep this simple."

I remembered earlier in his Warner Brother's office, he had said, "I am going to shoot each scene in 'Alice Doesn't Live Here Anymore' so that there is a parable behind each scene."

The next morning, I went into the bar & went up to Marty. He said, "This will be like Nick Adams in 'The Petrified Forest.'" I did not know the reference meaning, but I shook my head yes & said, "Okay."

He introduced me to Ellen Burstyn & then he took me to a table & added several lines to the scene. I had worked as a waiter in N.Y.C. when I was studying acting & so I understood the bartender character. I wore a navy blue shirt (western) & a white western tie that looked something like a cross. Levi's & cowboy boots also — Marty liked my costume.

Right before we began shooting, Marty came up to me & said, "I'm going to shoot this so that the red lights in the bar reflect off your blue shirt." Later, he added, "This is a close-up, so, do not move much." I thought, he has everything covered & that relaxed me.

The Hollywood Reporter ended its review of "Alice Doesn't Live Here Anymore" by saying "The acting of Harry Northup as 'Jim's & Joe's Bartender' exemplifies the emotional honesty of the cast."

Marty told me that my scene was the only one in the movie that was 1 to 1 — exactly on the screen as it was shot.

I love working with him. He's a preeminent American director.

"Taxi Driver" (1975)

Scorsese told me he wanted me to play "Doughboy." He handed me the script of "Taxi Driver" & said, "The dialogue's too direct; you know the way we work — sideways." I was in his office at The Burbank Studios. He added, "I'm going to shoot the city in such a surreal way no one ever has before. I'm going to turn 'Taxi Driver' into a gothic horror story."

A week later I was called by an assistant of Marty's & asked to come in & tape the part of "Travis Bickle" so they could send it to De Niro, who was doing "1900" in Italy, so that he could study my mid-west accent. I went in to the studio & read "Travis Bickle's" lines into a tape recorder.

I had four scenes in the movie. The first one was a 3-page scene that took place at the Bellmore Cafeteria, a cabbie hang-out on Park Avenue South.

The first night of shooting for me was on July 2, 1975. We had a rehearsal at Scorsese's room at the St. Regis Hotel at 6 P.M. & our call was at 8:45 P.M. We did the lines in the script, plus we improvised. Marty's assistant taped the scene, typed out the recording & he compressed the best & gave us the newly typed compression.

Marty was always very thorough, covering the scene from every angle, master, to two shots, singles, close-ups. In the beginning, I remember he came up behind me, put his hands on my shoulders in a very warm way & said, "Relax."

I remember his loving & laughing at my improvisations.

Once, someone brought a danish up to the table & put it between Marty & De Niro as we were all sitting there in between takes. They broke it in half & each ate half. They were half & half of the movie.

But, Marty always gave each character his/her own rich density in the film.

The second large scene that I was in was shot in a real cabbies' hang out on 45th & Tenth. It was a 6-page scene, also shot at night. De Niro entered the scene after we were there & Marty had him sit a chair away from me so that there was an oval gap in the middle-right part of the screen. Marty would rehearse Peter Boyle, myself & the other actor & then have De Niro come in during the actual shooting. He did not want De Niro to rehearse with us. Wanted to help create the alienation. Same thing with the Bellmore Cafeteria scene. Most of the dialogue in the scene was in the script, but I spiced mine up — "Got change for a nickel, Travis?" instead of "Yeah, we went to Harvard together," after "Wizard" had said, "Travis, you know Doughboy, Charlie T?"

This scene was about "You carry a piece? You need one?" "Well, you ever need one, I know a feller that kin get cha a real nice deal. Lots a shit around." Part of the action line of the script. Later on, I pick up "Travis" & introduce him to the gun salesman & drive them to the salesman's place where De Niro buys an arsenal.

The one thing that I did do that wasn't in the script was that I tried to sell De Niro a piece of Errol Flynn's bathtub. I told Marty my idea after rehearsing the scene. I said I would do it after I had exited the scripted scene. I would re-enter, pull the piece out of my pocket & try to sell it to him. If Marty didn't like it, he could cut it & still have the original scripted scene intact & he wouldn't have to move the camera for another set-up. Marty loved the idea. He told De Niro that I was going to try something at the end — try to sell him something & just say no. The scene was fabulous & off-beat. Later, I realised Marty's use of water images & it fit in.

Marty always loved it when actors tried something new. After the movie was over, he sent me a signed peuter cup with "Taxi Driver" 1975 & his name printed on it. "Taxi Driver" won the 1976 Palme d'Or at the Cannes Film Festival.

"New York, New York" (1976)

In 1976, I worked a week on "New York, New York," playing "Alabama" in an opening scene.

"Amazing Stories" (1985)

In 1985, I played a "Security Guard" in his first TV show, "Amazing Stories."

In 1989, I received an invitation to a screening of "Last Temptation Of Christ," at which Scorsese was to be honored by The Los Angeles Film Teachers with a first-ever-given award for courage. I met him & talked to him briefly in the theatre lobby. He was, as always, warm & kind to me.

August 2, 1991

MEDITATION ON
THE NEW AMERICAN POETRY

THE NEW AMERICAN POETRY, EDITED BY DONALD M. ALLEN, PUBLISHED BY GROVE PRESS, INC., 80 University Place, New York, NY 10003, 1960, 454 pages, $2.95.

I studied Method acting with Frank Corsaro in Manhattan from 1963-1968. In 1966, Lee Hickman, a student in the class, & I decided to do a scene together. One day, after rehearsal, he put a book in my hand. It was *THE NEW AMERICAN POETRY.* I took it home & read it.

The most important thing, to me, was that it brought poetry down to the ground. A person didn't have to be a college professor, or John Milton, or an intellectual to write poetry. A person could compose poesy from his, or her, own life. Using one's experience, one's imagination, one's memory. Just like Method acting. The gods in the roots of the trees, in the tips of the flowers, mystical visions seen on the subway.

It's now twenty-five years later & I have made my living as an actor for eighteen years, having acted in "Mean Streets," "Taxi Driver," "Over The Edge," "The Silence Of The Lambs," among others. And I have had five books of poetry published, including *ENOUGH THE GREAT RUNNING CHAPEL* & *the images we possess kill the capturing.*

There have been many sexual, political & social changes in the past quarter century. The most recent & most disturbing is the one involved with "political correctnesss, " a conforming to a tribe mentality, amounting to brutal censorship of the individual's right to freedom of speech.

I believe what America stands for is the individual. I do not believe in censorship.

I believe that *THE NEW AMERICAN POETRY* was a change in form in poetry. The new social, sexual, political movements have offered nothing new in form, much newness in content. The one new thing that has happened is "he, or she," instead of "he."

I was talking to Holly Prado about how important *TNAP* was to me & she said, "I remember how different the poetry on the page looked."

To me, the central American tradition in poetry stems from Whitman & Dickinson & continues through Pound, Eliot, Williams, Olson, Duncan, Ginsberg, Creeley. It is poetry pure & simple. It is not poetry used for political terms or sexual ones to bludgeon one's opponent, or a grasp for sexual or racial power.

It is with this personal & societal background that I have turned once again to rereading *THE NEW AMERICAN POETRY*. There are no victims washing themselves in this fountain. There is a love of language, a love of self, of experience, of study & of loss. A search for the real & the mystical. I sit at the edge of this fountain & wash my feet in it.

There are forty men & four women in *TNAP: 1945-1960*. The first poem is "The Kingfishers," by Charles Olson & it begins "What does not change / is the will to change." His second poem "I Maximus Of Gloucester, To You" is Olson's mythic attempt to forge an American epic. It begins "By ear, he sd." He continues later with "one loves only form," & "love is form, and cannot be without" echoing H.D.'s statement that without love there is no vision. Olson states "the HEAD, by way of the EAR, to the SYLLABLE / the HEART, by way of the BREATH, to the LINE." The other two famous phrases are "FORM IS NEVER MORE THAN AN EXTENSION OF CONTENT." "Phrased by...Creeley." And Dahlberg's "ONE PERCEPTION MUST IMMEDIATELY AND DIRECTLY LEAD TO A FURTHER PERCEPTION." "Open verse" & *composition by field* are also tantamount to Olson.

To me, it's more than Olson's projective verse poetics, the open form (Maximus poems, Pound's *The Cantos*, Zukofsky's *"A"*), as opposed to the closed form (*The Bridge*); it's more than Creeley's short-lined, taut breaths, rhythm, humanity; it's more than fast American-traipsed in cars, subways, drugs, paranoia, dissent, deep resonance of Ginsberg; more than Blackburn's real intersection, great counting of subway passengers: it's many stops, typewriter-written. What is the level of reality we are willing to accept?

I went to other books, many bought at the Eighth Street bookstore, *The Cities*, by Blackburn, Creeley's *For Love*, Dorn, O'Hara, Ginsberg. Something favoring the long, free poem, something giving short urban lyrics. Some anger, some freeing.

Looking at the number of women poets, in our time surely it would reflect more of a balance among men & women.

This is May, 1991, & I am totally blasted, I am broke, disaffiliated. Driving east on Fountain, I thought, "I am going to pull a robbery, or fuck a chick." But, I love my freedom, I respect the law & I don't want jail; my marriage will be one year old in several days. I respect my wife.

To get more, you have to get work. Deeper isolation does not get it.

Olson's Maximus epic derives from America's deepest tradition. The north-east where our Pilgrims arrived. The sea-going, shipbuilding, movement out into the sea for sustenances; the building of a city, like Greek times — a man also, where we came from, what is our language's tradition? How we have become separated from Europe, what have we held dear to, & continued?

I have attempted the long poem. It's like film as montage. Sometimes I think of film as whole montage. Building of images.

The facing of sins. We have built this country on the work ethic, religious values, a respect for the individual, "no discrimination because of race, color or creed."

To write clear & concise, to have rhythm. Much has been written about the jazz influences on many of these poets. This is the rhythm I have come out of. This book bridges Whitman, Pound, Williams to the civil rights era, women's movement, sorrow over Vietnam, the era of social, sexual, political acts attempting to balance public & private morality. Morality is the trust of law from all humans to honor life above death.

"I wake you, / stone. Love this man." Ends Olson. Dated 17 October 1959.

"—but from this threshold / it is age / that is beautiful. It is toward the old poets / we go, to their faltering, / their unaltering wrongness that has style, / their variable truth, / the old faces, / words shed like tears from / a plenitude of powers times stores." Duncan. He has a section in "A Poem Beginning With A Line By Pindar" dedicated to Olson, & begins "Psyche's tasks — the sorting of seeds." The poet's job. He ends with "In the dawn that is nowhere / I have seen the willful children / clockwise & counter-clockwise turning." The nuclear bomb explosion to end W.W. II was the image of deconstructionism.

Radiant good word. Levertov, in "Pleasures": "I like to find / what's not found / at once, but lies / within something of another nature, in repose, distinct... large enough to fill / the hungry palm of a hand."

("the seed.") "in the narrow flute from which the morning-glory / opens blue and cool on a hot morning." I remember Levertov writing how important Duncan was to her. I remember her lines "Each step / an arrival." Clean writing. Rhythmical. The language in this book seems very Puritanical, although obviously, there is much rebellion against it, a moving in to the American frontier night. "I like the juicy stem of grass that grows."

Blackburn, though a minor poet, was the one that influenced me the most. The son of a poet, Blackburn was a modern troubadour, an urban poet — he'd describe vividly an intersection, Tenth & Second. *The Cities*, Grove Press, one of my favorite books. He used the typewriter to its extreme. He wrote how he heard people speak. Humorous, dry, he writes about what he sees, what he hears, relationships, love, "to illuminate"; he makes lists "The tanned blonde / in the green print sack / in the center of the subway car / standing / though there are seats / has had it from / 1 teenage hood / 1 lesbian / 1 envious housewife / 4 men over fifty / (& myself), in short / the contents of this half of the car… She has us and we her / all the way to downtown Brooklyn / Over the tunnel and through the bridge / to DeKalb Avenue we go…"

Many of these are urban poets. Whitman, Baudelaire, Eliot before them. Blackburn & his subways, Ginsberg moving through the city on drugs.

Creeley, lean man, lean poems. The complete text of "The Warning": "For love — I would / split open your head and put / a candle in / behind the eyes. // Love is dead in us / if we forget / the virtues of an amulet / and quick surprise." A good poet in the tradition of Williams, Olson. American clarity of speech. He drives into the dark night American frontier where poets write to understand each other, a sharing of place, real outer & inner. The poems are the inner man. A construct that includes love & loneliness & a caring for others. He dedicates "The Door" to Duncan & "The Awakening" to Olson. "Oh well, I will say here, / knowing each man, / let you find a good wife too, / and love her as hard as you can." Creeley's last stanza in "The Way." Page 87 in a 454-page book. To note the journey across this American landscape.

Good clean American speech. I enjoyed reading Dorn's "Vaquero" again. It begins "The cowboy stands beneath / a brick-orange moon." & ends "Yi Yi, the cowboy's eyes / are blue. The top of the sky / is too."

Dorn's sense of American Place has also always been important to me.

Joel Oppenheimer's lower case, concise poems close the first of five sections in *TNAP*.

Yesterday, a Thursday, I watched an NBA play-off game from 10 A.M. to 12:30 P.M.; the "MacNeil/Lehrer NewsHour" at 3 P.M.; a half hour of "Wings" (1927), the first Best Film Production; "Crossfire" at 4:30 P.M.; NBC News at 6:30; an hour of another NBA game; "Pickpocket" (1959), directed by Robert Bresson. 75 minutes. 7 hours & 15 minutes of television.

This morning I got up & began rereading *TNAP*. Refreshing.

The first group of poets, Olson, Duncan, Creeley, Dorn, Oppenheimer, Williams, Blackburn, Carroll, Eigner, Levertov, were published in *Origin & Black Mountain Review*.

The second group was the San Francisco Renaissance. These poets lived mostly in the Bay Area.

The playful love ballad by Helen Adams & Brother Antonius' poems of reverence to God & his creatures open the second section.

Ferlinghetti ends "He" with the word "Death" twenty-nine times.

Robin Blaser: surface, death, desire, death, love, language.

Jack Spicer, in "Imaginary Elegies, I-IV," for Robin Blaser, begins "Poetry, almost blind like a camera / Is alive in sight only for a second... Lucky for us that there are visible things like oceans / Which are always around,..." Spicer's great.

I remember enjoying "After Anacreon," by Lew Welch. He makes poetry out of work: "When I drive cab / I bring the sailor home from the sea. In the back of / my car he fingers the pelt of his maiden." I still enjoy it.

In "Moon Is To Blood," Richard Duerden writes, "grounded, there is the pleasure of a toilet seat, after her, / an act / of warm respect. / Moon. Moon. To whom my hands are out. / When I turned to the room I saw that the woman sleeping / is half woman half bird. / At her sides there are long wings, folded."

Philip Lamantia, Surrealist, sings "Here's Charmed Bird, Zephyr of High Crags-jugs of the divine / poem / As it weaves terrestial spaces, overturning tombs, breaking / hymens..." in his "Morning Light Song."

We see the underground making strides across the page, wide steps, words falling off to the side below, cutting back to the left margin, a generous use of the typewriter. We see Ferlinghetti turning the middle-class values upside-down. We see a high linguistic intelligence in Spicer. Howls, sweeps, aches, pushing celebratory devotion toward God & poetry into middle-class America — all in a new & excellent visionary way of writing poetry.

"Venice Recalled," by Bruce Boyd is nice, "& the poem, what it means to say, / for the natural motion of its body, is the clearer / that remarks the wider movement of its actual thought."

Kirby Doyle's "Strange," an urban, existentialist poem.

Ebbe Borregaard, in "Some Stories of the Beauty Wapiti," writes these dense lines: "in montalto with tonio by leoncavallo / pia mater delicate membrane peach pink in wine vagabonda / here before the inconsolate wapiti is wine mingled with myrrh…"

Lee Hickman died Sunday, May 12, 1991, at 6:30 A.M. In 1966, Lee & I were studying acting in Manhattan with Frank Corsaro. He is presently the head of Actors Studio. Lee & I decided to do a scene together. We did a short story about a Madison Avenue guy who picks up a 42nd St. hustler. I played the hustler. After arriving at his apartment, I asked him to make me a martini & have him wash my feet. He got a pillow for my feet & washed my feet. It was the first time a man washed my feet & the awakened feelings worked for the scene.

One day we were rehearsing at his studio downtown on the west side. He had a bookcase full of nothing but poetry. He put *THE NEW AMERICAN POETRY* in my hand. Loaned it to me. I bought a copy of my own.

Section III: The Beats: Kerouac (1922), Ginsberg (1926), Corso (1930), Orlovsky (1933). Kerouac's "183rd Chorus": "Only awake to Universal Mind / And realize that there is nothing / Whatever to be attained. This / Is the real Buddha." A quote to begin. It's last stanza: "Only awake to Universal Mind, / accept everything, / see everything, / it is empty, / Accept as thus — the Truth."

Ginsberg's famous "Sunflower Sutra." "You were never no locomotive, Sunflower, you were a sunflower!" "Howl, Parts I And II" for Carl Solomon: "I saw the best minds of my generation destroyed by madness…" "What does that line mean?" an interviewer asked Ginsberg. "It means, I saw the best minds of my generation destroyed by madness," Allen replied. The long, rolling, Blakean visionary lines. Urban, rebellious, burning, drugged, sexual. Rages against materialist America. Love for Neal. Later, pages of "Kaddish," his second great work, his first, "Howl." Ginsberg 24 pages, Olson 38 pages, O'Hara 32 pages. Duncan 20 pages. Ginsberg has the deepest resonance, back through Blake, Shakespeare, to the Old Testament prophets, Isaiah, Jeremiah, Micah. I remember being handed a copy of "Howl" in the basement apartment of an art student at Nebraska State Teachers College, Kearney. I was acting in "The Great God Brown" & he was working on the sets, painting. I remember the powerful, serpentine lines. That was in the fall of 1962. "...who chained themselves to subways for the endless ride from / Battery to holy Bronx on benzedrine... who let themselves be fucked in the ass by saintly motorcyclists, / and screamed with joy..." These last two lines I had never seen in a poem. "Moloch whose blood is / running money." A litany in chants.

There is a desire to go fast because these poems are so familiar. But no, I am going to stop & go slow, read each poem carefully & try to articulate my thoughts, first hand. Now & then. Death. The deaths they had lived with in the Second World War.

His magnificent "Kaddish," parts of it. "Strange now to think of you, gone without corsets and eyes, while / I walk on the sunny pavement of Greenwich Village / ... and I've been up all / night, talking, talking, reading the Kaddish aloud,... and Naomi — to God's perfect Darkness — Death, stay thy / phantoms!...'The key is in the sunlight at the window in the bars the key is / in the sunlight,'... Lord Lord Lord caw caw caw Lord Lord Lord caw caw caw Lord." Through Shakespeare & Biblical. I see Hickman coming out of Ginsberg — its long, sinewy line.

Corso, the angel-hipster. Shelly-like & criminal-like, & humorous "Birthplace Revisited." He gets into a poetry alone. Drugs. Surreal fun with poetic phrases out of a real line. "Marriage": "...Do you take this woman / for your lawful wedded wife? / And I, trembling what to say, say Pie Glue!... But I should get married I should be good / How nice it'd be to come home to her / and sit by the fireplace and she in the kitchen / aproned young and lovely wanting my baby / ... No! I should not get married I should never get married!" His ins & outs, dreams, vulnerabilities continue in this beautiful, fun poem (1959). Almost at a transitional time — change with the institution of marriage.

Peter Orlovsky's "Second Poem" ends this section. "For this drop of time upon my eyes / like the endurance of a red star on a cigarette / makes me feel life splits faster than scissors." Its last three lines: "I was born to remember a song about love — on a hill a butterfly / makes a cup that I drink from, walking over a bridge of / flowers." "Nov. '57, Paris."

Very beautiful poetry by Barbara Guest begins Section IV. The airy & light "Parachutes, My Love, Could Carry Us Higher." A stanza from "Sunday Evening": "Barges on the river carry apples wrapped in bales, / This morning there was a sombre sunrise, / In the red, in the air, in what is falling through us / We quote several things." In "Santa Fe Trail," the "I go separately," poignant. Her "Piazzas" ends: "when the air is clear of shadows / and no one walks the piazza." Lucid, graceful poetry. A nice surprise.

I like James Schuyler, in particular "Salute" & "February." Lean, graceful.

Koch's "Fresh Air" contains humor, irreverence, vitality, parody. Long lines, almost prose-like.

The three poets who were important to me in my beginning are dead: Lee Hickman, Paul Blackburn, Ann Stanford. Lee handed me *THE NEW AMERICAN POETRY* & reading it turned me on to other books, one being *The Cities*, by Blackburn. Hickman May 12, 1991; Ann Stanford 1987, I believe. Blackburn 1971.

Frank O'Hara's poems include "For James Dean," "Why I Am Not A Painter," "In Memory of My Feelings," "Ode To Joy," "Ode: Salute To The French Negro Poets," "Ode To Michael Goldberg...," "The Day Lady Died." I list them to cite some of his subject matters. "The Day Lady Died" begins "It is 12:20 in New York a Friday / three days after Bastille Day, yes / it is 1959 and I go get a shoeshine / because I will get off the 4:19 in Easthampton / at 7:15 and then go straight to dinner / and I don't know the people who will feed me..." It ends "and a NEW YORK POST with her face on it / and I am sweating a lot by now and thinking of / leaning on the john door in the FIVE SPOT / while she whispered a song along the keyboard / to Mel Waldron and everyone and I stopped breathing." An elegant, urban poet who wrote as he worked & walked — among artists, down Fifth, a lover of charisma & movie stars & jazz greats & the art world. Many levels of elegance. Real down-to-earth, also in talk.

John Ashberry's three poems end Section IV.

There are eleven poets in Section V. Philip Whalen & Gary Snyder I admire very much. Ray Bremser is also a favorite of mine.

"Love is better than hate" is repeated three times by "The sacred beasts" in Whalen's "Martyrdom of Two Pagans." Nine times he uses the word "love" in the fluently fast, musical "2 Variations: All About Love." This poem & the next, "Sourdough Mountain Lookout" are two favorites of mine. From "Sourdough...": "I always say I won't go back to the mountains / I am too old and fat there are bugs mean mules / And pancakes every morning of the world... Outside the lookout I lay nude on the granite / Mountain hot September sun but inside my head / Calm dark night with all the other stars... I keep telling myself what I really like / Are music, books, certain land and sea-scapes / The way light falls across them, diffusion of / Light through agate, light itself... I suppose / I'm still afraid of the dark... Like they say, 'Four times up, / Three times down.' I'm still on the mountain." From "For C.": "I wanted to bring you this Jap iris / Orchid-white with yellow blazons... If you were out, I'd leave these flowers. / Even if I couldn't write or speak / At least I broke and stole that branch with love." Whalen's poetry, full of love & humor & wisdom, still moves me.

There is something life-affirming in this anthology — Ginsberg, Whalen, Snyder, Kerouac. Maybe living through W.W. II & then enjoying America in post-war American glory. '47, '48 could have been our high point — the Allied victory naturally the high point, but in after-glow. & these poets going up against the conventional. Many poems about death & poems with the word god. There seemed to be a connection with their creator — not trying to attack others in an effort to gain social, sexual, political power. They gave us a Romantic taste.

"found only hope that came from the realisation of the cleansing / & purification of pain," wrote Stuart Z. Perkoff in his search for an understanding of "why the six million had died." The only answer was hope said the wise man about his fasting & prayers in his search for knowledge — "he had no answer" only the cleansing & purifying held hope. "clothing these six million in my sins / & thrusting them in their foreign wrappings / into the flaming mouths of agony." Perkoff's poem "Feasts Of Death, Feasts Of Love" is basically a love poem containing death, asking for creation as opposed to destruction.

Gary Snyder — "a beauty like season or tide." "Riprap" begins, "Lay down these words / Before your mind like rocks. / placed solid, by hands / In choice of place, set / Before the body of the mind / in space and time: / Solidity of bark, leaf, or wall / riprap of things:...."

From "Burning": "One moves continually with the consciousness / Of that other, totally alien, non-human: / Humming inside like a taut drum, / Carefully avoiding any direct thought of it, / Attentive to the real-world flesh and stone... The Mother whose body is the Universe / Whose breasts are Sun and Moon, / the statue of Prajna / From Java: the quiet smile, / The naked breasts. / 'Will you still love me when my / breasts get big?' / the little girl said — // 'Earthly Mothers and those who suck / the breasts of earthly mothers are mortal — / but deathless are those who have fed / at the breast of the Mother of the Universe'... wet rocks buzzing / rain and thunder southwest / hair, beard, tingle / wind whips bare legs / we should go back / we don't... Hiked eighteen hours, finally found / A snag and a hundred feet on fire:... The mountains are your mind... The sun is but a morning star" —these pieces show Snyder's interest in nature, balance, quest for wisdom, attempts to unlock the primitive, love, Buddhism, metaphor found in real things, precise naming & human movement through nature, rhythm dictated by work in "Riprap."

I once told Ann Stanford that I thought Gary Snyder was his generation's Robert Frost. She said, "Snyder is better than Frost."

Edward Marshall's eleven page poem "Leave The Word Alone" includes this near the end: "It is a painful process but it is a process I must go through / to stay out of the asylum..." He faces the pain of crazyness in his family & in himself & writes about it, instead of avoiding it by denial.

McClure has eighteen energetic pages. Often a line will be all in caps.

In his "Poem of Holy Madness, Part IV," Ray Bremser writes "but I love / the visionary out of jail, / that spectral escape that screws the federal / government! / I would prefer to run around with tramps, / and homosexual cats in drag rather than suck / the tinfoil tits of brittle broads / born in Nebraska!... and I dig jazz, / and hipsters,..." & ends "those hooves / come all / galloping headlong into the soft-spoken kiss / of the poets / whose sad skinny banners / were long-ago verbs / that had long-ago moved / so much more than mere mankind / to gestures, / and love!"

Amiri Baraka (Leroi Jones) writes about listening to the radio in "In Memory of Radio." "Who has ever stopped to think of the divinity of Lamont Cranston?... Saturday mornings we listened to *Red Lantern* & his undersea folk. / At 11, *Let's Pretend* / & we did / & I, the poet, still do, Thank God!"

In "To A Publisher... cut-out," he writes, "But who am I to love anybody? I ride the 14th St. bus / everyday... reading Hui neng/ Raymond Chandler/Olson... / I have slept with almost every medicore colored woman / On 23rd St.... At any rate, talked a good match."

In "A Poem For Painters," John Wieners writes "My poems contain no / wilde beestes, no / lady of the lake, music / of the spheres, / or organ chants. / Only the score of a man's / struggle to stay with / what is his own, what / lies within him to do. / Without which is nothing. / And I come to this / knowing the waste, / leaving the rest up to love / and its twisted faces, / my hands claw out at / only to draw back from the / blood already running there." Wieners: homosexuality, heroin, love & loss & hunger & sadness.

Ron Loewinsohn & David Meltzer finish the poem section of the book. There are also "Statements on Poetics" & "Biographical Notes."

A singing of what these people are, where they come from, the land they roam over, a use of drugs, a seeking of wisdom, camaraderie, compassion.

It is still my favorite poetry anthology.

November 8, 1991

released friday night eleven-thirty: "hero"

he's a great director, strong, clear
shock of black hair, brooding, thinking, decisive
commands
in a way, it's like being part of the words
watching a great novelist creating, making it
come alive
220 people cast & crew that night
35 drivers
bridge plane crash lake heroics
a canterbury tales journey
disastrous times but with hope

scene father reading a magazine
son playing a video game
father looks at son & smiles
scene father his head turned to the left
sleeping also son with head on father's right shoulder
beep seat belt on captain's voice comes on
father puts his seat belt on puts son's on son wakes him
looks around at other passengers looks out window
puts his arm around the son & holds him
scene tv interviewer asks & father answers
"perfect" said stephen
a little more empasis on "the man" "that i was still
in there"

the conciseness & clarity
movies to me are like fiction used to be
november 22 - december 13
a week in january
happy to be working with a great director
i have seen four of his films & each one is different
"too big," he said to me right before i entered a scene
"this film is too big."

a scene where the father reunites with his son
"this is a difficult scene to shoot," stephen said
fires on the plane people in the lake people coming
up the hill firemen running many criss-cross ways
it seemed but in the rain & the fire trucks sirens lights
reflections mud mayhem there was order & the father
picked the son up & later crossed in front of the hero
walked toward the camera a little to the right toward
the red flashing light then a tracking shot of the hero
a cop a woman asking for help takes the hero another way
to see it come to life to be a small part a character
develops my job was the father-son relation
it is two days later i feel it is an honor to work
in a stephen frears film

12   15   91

z

whole god kingdom nuclear weapon the seed of deconstructionism

a movie that made $190 million world wide & got 85-90% great
reviews

cahuenga press publishes its second volume of poetry

4 weeks work in a movie directed by stephen frears
1 week in a psychological thriller

removing sentiment requires taking out the personal just facts
bone words without the human

a movie about an eskimo lesbian who's attracted to a german
middle-aged widow librarian
a movie about young male hustlers
audio works for mobile society

1 year & 7 months married
son works washington & lincoln 2 years

"personal crime," selected & new poems 1966-1991
poet who turned me on to poetry 25 years died a.i.d.s.

8 a.m. she gets out of bed goes to the bathroom comes back
climbs into bed naked
they kiss he rubs her ass her thighs her back her breasts
belly inner thigh he finger fucks her he tongues her cunt
she sucks his cock he gets on top of her & they fuck his
mouth is wet

a front-page sunday book review story on a celebration of 40
years small presses in los angeles 19 editors men & women

the bone broken in two places & the boy limped when he first
walked without crutches now there is no limp now the boy
surfs whenever he can whenever he's off work & there are some
good waves
straight down the street from his house bay street

his eyes chose six bells
the 19th year he has made a moderate income from acting in
the movies

5 nights in a motel across from magic mountain lobster fire rain
wide golden leaf fallen & picked up nature admired
tree barren of leaves on northwest side near road leaves on other
side

12   27   91

Harry E. Northup has had five previous books of poetry published. Of *the images we possess kill the capturing*, the eminent critic Robert Peters wrote, "No poet has written more movingly about the vicissitudes of professional acting—" (*small press review*, Nov., 1991). Northup received his B.A. in English from California State University, Northridge, where he studied with the poet Ann Stanford. He has made a living as an actor for twenty-one years, acting in thrity-three films, including Scorsese's first six films ("Mean Streets" & "Taxi Driver," among them). Jonathan Demme has hired him for eight acting roles, including "Mr. Bimmel" in "The Silence Of The Lambs." He starred in "Fighting Mad" & "Over The Edge." Recently, he acted in "Bad Girls" & "Reform School Girl" for Jonathan Kaplan. New Alliance Records has released his "Personal Crime," new and selected poems from 1966-1991 on CD & cassette audio recording, & "Homes" on CD.

Michael Arkush, writing in *The Los Angeles Times*, said, "For Northup, his dual life as an actor and poet gives him a perfect blend of the make-believe and the real-life introspection he thrives on in his poetry."

He lives in Los Angeles with his wife, Holly Prado Northup. His son Dylan is twenty-six years old.